QUARRY

QUARRY

A "Nameless Detective" Mystery

by

BILL PRONZINI

**Delacorte
Press**

Published by
Delacorte Press
Bantam Doubleday Dell Publishing Group, Inc.
666 Fifth Avenue
New York, New York 10103

Library of Congress Cataloging in Publication Data
Pronzini, Bill.
    Quarry: a "nameless detective" mystery/by Bill Pronzini.
      p.   cm.
    ISBN 0-385-30519-2 (hc): $18.00
    I. Title.
PS3566.R67Q37   1992
813'.54—dc20   91-15284
                                                             CIP

Manufactured in the United States of America
Published simultaneously in Canada

January 1992

10 9 8 7 6 5 4 3 2 1
BVG

For Bruce Taylor and Steve Stilwell,
the Mutt and Jeff of mystery booksellers,
one of whom has impeccable taste

So perhaps we are in hell,
For all that I can tell,
And lost, and damned,
And served up hot to God.

—JOHN DAVIDSON

Chapter **1**

COOL, WINDY MONDAY in late April. Pale sun, scattered cumulus clouds. Nice day for a long, solitary drive into the country, especially when you had a partner and best friend who was getting married in a few days and who was turning everyone concerned into basket cases with his prenuptial mania. . . .

There wasn't much traffic on Highway 101 south of King City, and when I turned off at San Lucas there was no traffic at all. The sleepy village with its huge, dead storage silos seemed deserted; so did Cattlemen Road leading out of it to the south; so did the vineyards and produce fields that flanked the two-lane blacktop. It was as if all the people had gone somewhere else—as if I were passing through Hamelin Town not long after the piper's visit.

But then, except for the harvest season, it was always like this down here in the central part of the state. Anybody who thinks California is just one big string of cities and suburbs, wall-to-wall people from one end to the other, has never driven through the southern reaches of the Salinas Valley, between King City and Paso Robles a hundred and fifty miles southeast of San Francisco. This is Steinbeck country: the setting of *East of Eden* and the stories in *The Long Valley*. Earthquake country: the San Andreas and Rinconada faults run right through it. Agricultural country: the "salad bowl of America," where lettuce is known as "green gold" and broccoli, beets, wine grapes, and a dozen other crops flourish under the hot summer sun. Or used to flourish, before the winter rains began to disappear a few years ago; now the worst drought in a century held the Central Coast area in its dusty thrall.

This was Old California, too, a part of the state that has changed hardly at all over the past half century and remarkably little since the 1840s, when this was a thirteen-thousand-acre Mexican land grant called the San Bernado Rancho. The little farm towns—San Lucas, San Bernado, San Ardo, Bradley, San Miguel—look much as they did in Steinbeck's day; so do the fields, the farms and ranches, the rolling hills that stretch away to the Santa Lucia Range to the east and lift into the Gabilan Range to the west. You can even see, without looking too hard, sagging barns with Mail Pouch tobacco signs painted on their roofs and sides. Only the oil fields south of San Ardo and the four lanes of Highway 101 snaking through serve as reminders that this is the last decade of the twentieth century. Otherwise, coming here is like traveling into the past, when a kinder, gentler way of life was a reality and not a politician's wet dream.

Yeah, I told myself wryly, and coming here turns *you* into a knee-jerk sentimentalist with blinders on. The past wasn't so damn great, buddy boy. Ask one of the survivors of the Dust Bowl migration in the thirties; he'll tell you about the good old days. Steinbeck, too, if you bother to reread him.

But it wasn't much of an argument; the pragmatic and cynical side of me never has stood much of a chance against the old-fashioned side. I'm a throwback—the kind of man who hates progress, mistrusts technology, and never quite feels comfortable in any place where he can't see or touch some small piece of the past. I *liked* being here in the Salinas Valley, drought or no drought; it made me feel good because I had a sense of belonging. So why should I apologize for romanticizing it a little? And to myself, for God's sake!

You're nuts, that's why, I thought. Throwback schizoid in a schizoid world, and content to be that way. Like one of the guys in the story about the bookstore browser who comes across a volume called *The Dual Personality* and says to the clerk, "You know, part of me wants to buy this and part of me doesn't." And the clerk says, "Buy it—it's the gospel truth and it'll change your life. On the other hand, it's probably bullshit and you don't really want to know anyway."

Cattlemen Road unwound straight and empty. Until the freeway was built in the sixties, it had been part of the main highway through this part of the valley; now it was just a patched-up back road, paralleled by railroad tracks on the east, the narrow, winding Salinas River and then the highway a half mile to the west. The bottomland here was mostly planted in wine grapes, lettuce, and beets. Beyond the railroad right-of-way, fields and sparse cattle graze sloped up to the Santa Lucia foothills—low gray-brown mounds, barren except for patches of dry grass and sage, their sides scored with deep puckered creases, like great blobs of clay that had been tossed down as part of some master sculpting plan and then inexplicably abandoned.

Men worked here and there among the grapevines and green vegetables. From a distance they might have been emigrants from the Depression-era Southwest; even the scattered pickups and other vehicles had an ancient, dusty look, like the truck the Joads had driven from Oklahoma to California. But when you got close enough, the illusion vanished. The men were all Mexican migrants, too many of them underpaid illegals. Time had changed, all right—but only on the surface. The exploitation was the same as it had been fifty years ago; it was only the faces and skin tones of the exploited that were different.

I covered five miles before I encountered another moving

car—a big dump truck loaded with gravel, swinging out of an unpaved road that snaked back into the hills. A sign at the intersection said that the side road led to the South Valley Gravel Company. It was also my landmark, the one that told me I was a mile outside San Bernado and a quarter of a mile from Arlo Haas's farm.

You couldn't miss his place, he'd told me on the telephone; it was the only one between the gravel company road and the outskirts of town. I turned in at the open gate and bumped up over the railroad tracks. On the north, then, stood a windbreak of eucalyptus trees; on the south, a rickety barbed-wire fence, along which tumbleweeds were caught like dry brown corpses in an abandoned web. Until a few years ago, Arlo Haas had said, the fields that stretched out on both sides had been planted in beets. Now the ones to the north, leased to a local winery, nurtured vineyards; the ones to the south lay fallow. Ahead, the farm buildings—house, barn, a couple of storage sheds, an unstable-looking windmill—were arranged against a long ravinelike crease where the nearest of the barren hills came together.

Beyond the house, an extension of the farm road curled up the side of one hill and over its crest. As I neared the farmyard, I noticed movement up there—somebody on foot, coming along the road from the other side. A woman, I thought; I could make out long, dark hair blowing wild in the wind. Grady Haas? She stopped abruptly, leaning forward, and stood poised for a few seconds, watching my approach. Then she was gone, back the way she'd come. Not walking—almost running.

Yeah, I thought. Grady Haas.

The house was at least three quarters of a century old—two-storied, with a pillared gallery at the second-floor level. It had once been painted a dark red, but the red had faded to the color of dusty brick; the white trim was flaked and faded as well. It reminded me of one of the old stage depots that still stand in remote corners of the West. Fronting it was a lattice-fenced yard that had once contained flower beds and a lawn; now there was nothing much in it except dead grass, over which ancient oaks and willows cast their shade.

The farmyard was deserted—no cars, no machinery, no animals or fowl. When I stopped the car and shut off the engine, I could hear a dog barking inside the house; otherwise, the wind had the area to itself and was making the most of it with blustery and meaningless noises. I went through an archway in the fence and onto a creaky porch under the gallery. I was reaching out to knock when the door opened and two pairs of eyes peered out at me.

One pair belonged to a big black dog with a massive head. The other pair were sunken deeply in the seamed and oddly lopsided face of a man about sixty—Arlo Haas. Tucked under his left armpit and supporting most of his weight was a metal crutch; in his right hand was the dog's collar. The animal strained against his grip, all hungry-eyed and slobbery, as if it would like nothing better than to have me for lunch. Its tail was wagging and it didn't look particularly vicious, but I was not taking anything for granted. I'd had run-ins with canines before; I hadn't won yet, and I had no desire for any new matches.

Haas allowed as how he appreciated my getting here a half hour early, it being only twelve-thirty. I didn't have the heart to tell him I was early by accident, not design. His voice had a raw, forced quality, as if it hurt him to talk. Maybe it did. His face seemed lopsided at first glance because the left side was stiff and withered, the result of a stroke he'd suffered four years ago. The stroke had mostly paralyzed his left hip and leg and retarded the use of his left arm. It was the reason he was no longer a beet farmer and had leased part of his land to the winery. It was also the reason he wanted to hire me to do a job he would have undertaken himself if he were able-bodied; and one of the reasons I'd agreed, at the end of his call early this morning, to drive down here and discuss the matter in detail. The other reasons were that I'd had nothing pressing to keep me in the city today, he'd offered to pay me for my time whether I went to work for him or not, and he'd appealed to my ego by saying that from what he'd read about me in the papers, I was the kind of "grass-roots detective" who would understand his problem.

He saw me still eyeing the dog and said, "Don't worry, he don't bite. But he'll climb strangers if I don't keep a hand on him. His name's Gus. Hell of a name for a pooch, but he come to me with it. You know much about dogs?"

"Not much."

"Labrador's what he is. Good breed, Labs."

"I'll take your word for it, Mr. Haas."

"Well, come on inside," he said. "Grady's not here and my housekeeper don't come in on Mondays."

He turned and hobbled away into the house, still hanging on to Gus's collar. I kept my distance just the same. The Lab walked with its head swiveled back my way, with that hungry look still in its eyes; maybe it didn't bite, but it wanted to do something to me—climb me or dry-hump me or pee on my leg. Just which was a mystery I didn't want solved.

The room we went into was a big old-fashioned parlor. Faded flower-patterned wallpaper, faded carpet, faded furniture, faded oil paintings and mostly faded family photographs in gilt frames. The only modern thing in it was a television set. But it managed nonetheless to be a pleasant, comfortable room brightened by sunlight that intruded through one of two big windows.

Haas said, "I got a pot of coffee made. Or maybe you want something cold?"

"Don't trouble yourself, Mr. Haas."

"No trouble. I could use another cup myself."

"All right, then. Black for me, no sugar. I can help if you want. . . ."

"No." He said the word almost curtly, with his eyes on mine; he was a proud man and he wanted me to know it. "Sit down, make yourself at home. Anywhere except the rocker."

He took the dog with him when he went out. The thump of his crutch and the clicking of the Lab's nails were faint, cheerless sounds in the early afternoon quiet.

I started toward a hirsute brown couch, changed my mind, and went to look at the photographs on the wall. There were half a dozen of Grady Haas, from infancy to womanhood, all of them candid shots and all apparently taken here. The most recent was no more than a couple of years old. It was of the two of them, father and daughter, him leaning on his crutch, her with her arm around his shoulders, smiling at each other. In the background was a tabletop Christmas tree, a scant few presents arranged under it. She was of average height, slender, darker than her father, attractive in a subtle way. Her most striking feature was her hair—thick blue-black waves of it that flowed over her shoulders and halfway down her back. There was affection in her smile, and she might have been having an enjoyable holiday visit, but there was something remote and solemn about her just the same, as if part of her was somewhere else.

"Pretty, ain't she?"

I turned. Haas had come back, balancing a tray with two cups of coffee on it in his right hand. The dog wasn't with him; he'd closed it into one of the other rooms. I heard it whine and then its nails click again as it began to pace around.

I said, "Yes, she's very pretty," and curbed an impulse to relieve him of the tray. He set it down on a table next to a heavy old rocker with padded arms and extra cushions, told me to help myself, then lowered his crippled body slowly into the rocker. One of the two coffee cups had his first name imprinted on it; I took the other one to the couch.

"Older she gets," he said when I was settled, "the better looking she gets. She was kind of gangly as a child."

"How old is she now?"

"Thirty-one. Her mother was like that too—pretty but gangly when I married her at twenty, beautiful by the time she was thirty-five. Still beautiful at forty-five, even with the cancer eating at her." He stopped talking and his eyes went blank for a few seconds; then he shook his head, touched the withered side of his face, lowered his hand. "God's been hard on this family," he said, but without bitterness.

I tasted my coffee before I said, "I saw somebody up on the hill road behind the house as I was driving in. Grady?"

"Yeah. Spends half her time in the hills since she come home."

"What's back there?"

"Cattle graze, or was when we kept cattle. Nothing now except a dry creek and more hills, and the gravel outfit over north."

"What does she do, then?"

He shrugged. "Just wanders. Same as when she was young, always off by herself. My wife called her Little Miss Lonesome. But hell, Grady was never unhappy. Just preferred her own company. Still does. That's why her coming home like this, all of a sudden, don't make any sense."

"She's never done that before?"

"Never. Comes down every year to spend Christmas, and once in a while on my birthday in August, if she can get away. Always calls a couple of days ahead to let me know she's coming. Not this time. No warning at all. Just showed up bright and early last Friday morning."

"How early?"

"Eight-thirty. She must of left the city around five."

"She give you any reason?"

"No. Didn't say much of anything, except she'd been working too hard and needed some time to herself, and would I mind if she stayed a week or two. Wouldn't look me in the eye when she said it. Never could look you in the eye when she was telling a lie, no matter how small."

"And you think she's in some kind of trouble."

"Don't think it," Haas said, "I know it. You can't always tell what's going on inside that girl; she hides her feelings pretty good. But she can't hide a thing like this. She's in shock. All busted up inside and in shock."

"Afraid?"

"That too. At least, I thought so when I first seen her."

"But not now?"

"No. Now she seems . . . I don't know, like she's resigned, like she don't care anymore."

"You have no idea what might have happened to her?"

"None. Mary Ellen couldn't get a hint out of her neither."

"Mary Ellen?"

"Mary Ellen Crowley. Used to be Mary Ellen Higgins. Grady's best friend when they were kids. Schoolteacher now, at the union school in San Bernado. I called her yesterday, asked her to come over. Grady wouldn't hardly talk to her. And after Mary Ellen left, she asked me not to tell anybody else she was back home. Didn't want to see or talk to anybody except me, she said."

"She hasn't had any other visitors, then?"

"No."

"How about calls?"

"No."

"Has she made any calls?"

"Not that I know of."

"Been off the property at any time since Friday?"

"You mean in her car? No, not even into town. She put that little car of hers in the barn when she got here and hasn't been near it since." He paused. "I went out and looked inside yesterday morning, while she was in the hills. Ain't nothing in it give me a clue to her trouble."

I had my notebook out now, open on one knee; but so far there hadn't been anything for me to write down. I asked, "I take it Grady's not married?"

"No."

"Has she ever been married?"

"No." He said the word a little sadly this time, as if the fact were a source of disappointment to him. Or maybe the disappointment lay in a lack of grandchildren to help ease his lonely existence. He'd told me on the phone that Grady was an only child.

"Does she have a steady boyfriend?"

"Had one a while last year. I thought it might be serious, but when I asked her to bring him down with her at Christmas, she said she wasn't seeing him anymore."

"Did she say why?"

"No. Just that they broke up."

"What's his name?"

"Ted? Todd? Something like that. I don't remember his last name. Mary Ellen might know."

"What does he do for a living?"

"Grady didn't tell me. And I didn't want to pry."

"You ever meet him in person?"

"Never met any of her boyfriends since high school," Haas said. "What few she's had. Never any she wanted me to meet."

"What about her female friends?"

"You mean up in the city? No, I never met any of them neither. Two times I went up to visit her, before my stroke, it was just the two of us." He shook his head again, reached for his coffee cup. "Real private, that girl," he said. "Guess I never give much thought to how private, until these past few days."

"Where does she live in San Francisco?"

"On Temescal Terrace, near the university."

"University of San Francisco or S.F. State?"

"U.S.F."

"She lives alone, is that right? No roommate?"

"Alone. Never had a roommate, even when she was in school."

"What's the street number?"

"Nine-eight-seven."

I made a note of the address.

He said when I was done writing, "I got a key."

"Key?"

"To her apartment. She give it to me the last time I visited her. Never asked for it back."

". . . You want me to go there and snoop around?"

"First thing I'd do," he said. "You got my permission."

"Legally you don't have the right to give permission."

"Hell, I'm her father."

"Doesn't matter. It's her home, not yours."

"Might be something there that'll tell what's troubling her." There was frustration in his heavy voice now. He wasn't interested in his daughter's personal affairs for any nosy paternal reason; he was genuinely worried about her. "I'll take responsibility. I'll put it in writing that it was all my idea."

I sighed, not too audibly. "We're getting ahead of ourselves, Mr. Haas. Some more questions first, all right?"

He drew a deep breath and let it out slow before he said, "All right."

"Did Grady attend U.S.F.?"

"Four years. Got her degree in business administration, graduated in the top five percent of her class. She's smart, Grady is—real smart." She'd given him that much to hang his pride on, at least.

"She works in the city, does she?"

"Intercoastal Insurance. Been with them since her graduation. Got promoted to assistant chief adjuster in their damage claims department a couple of years ago."

In my profession you get to know the insurance companies pretty well, particularly the small ones; they can't afford to employ full-time investigative staffs, so they farm out that kind of work to private agencies like mine. Intercoastal was a newish outfit based in L.A.; their San Francisco office specialized in marine and marine-industry insurance. Rumor had it that they were not the most financially stable of companies these days.

I said, "Could be she's having some kind of work-related problem. Maybe even lost her job for internal reasons. That would explain her suddenly wanting to come home for a while, give herself time to regroup."

"Wouldn't explain her being tore up like this," Haas said. "Losing her job wouldn't do that to her, not Grady. Anyhow, I thought of that myself. So I called up Intercoastal Insurance this morning, before I called you. She ain't been fired, don't have any problems at work. She had some vacation time coming and she asked for it and they give it to her, that's all."

"Who'd you talk to at Intercoastal?"

"Her assistant. Seems even assistants got assistants in their damage claims department."

"Who would that be?"

"Lisa Fisher."

I wrote the name down in my notebook. When I looked at Haas again, he was staring at something or someone not in this room. The patch of sunlight coming through the window on his left had lengthened so it touched the withered side of his face, giving it a pale radiance. Gus was still moving restlessly at the rear of the house. I could hear the wind, too, playing tag with itself among the shade trees outside.

Abruptly Haas blinked and focused on me again. "The thing that happened to her . . . it ain't as simple as something wrong at work. It's bad trouble, the kind that rips up your insides. You know what I mean?"

"I think so, yes."

"Somebody did that to her," he said. "Tore her up that way, tore her up so bad she may never be the same again. I ain't exaggerating about that."

I nodded and said nothing.

"Got it locked up inside her, whatever it is, like poison in a jar. I want to help her, but she just won't let me get at it, won't let nobody get at it. That's why I need you."

I stayed silent, thinking about her up there on the hill— hunched against the wind, her hair blowing wild around her, then turning and hurrying away, back to where there was nothing but barren earth and empty sky. I had been torn up myself not so long ago, and alone with my pain for three terrible months, and during that time I would have given anything to have people around me; even now, more than a year later, there were days when I needed the closeness of crowds. But Grady Haas was just the opposite. She embraced solitude and in a crisis retreated even more deeply inside herself. Still, she was chained to the person or thing that had damaged her, just as I had been chained for ninety-seven days to the wall of an isolated mountain cabin.

Her father mistook my silence for indecision. He said with as much pleading as he would ever be able to muster, "I got to know what's going on so I can help her get shut of it. I *got* to. You can understand that, can't you?"

"I understand, Mr. Haas."

"She's all I got left," he said.

There was no way I could refuse him, even if I'd been inclined that way. I told him what he wanted to hear. And watched the keen edge of his anxiety slowly dull. And thought again of her up there on the hill—Little Miss Lonesome, running away.

Chapter **2**

SAN BERNADO was like something caught on a snag in the river of time. The snag was 1940, and all the years since seemed to have flowed around and away from it without touching it except at the edges. There was nothing illusory about its look and feel of the past; it was an actual physical anachronism that even smelled a little musty and dusty, like something old and lost and mostly forgotten. Even the few modern touches—cars, trucks, house trailers, satellite dishes— seemed to have a washed-out, prematurely aged look, as if the town had bled their newness out of them while absorbing them into its time-snagged persona.

Back before the bypassing freeway was built, when Highway 101 passed right through San Bernado, it had had activity and a certain energy; now, thirty years later and on a Monday afternoon in April, it was all but deserted and wore a somnolent air that was probably perpetual. The business section was three blocks long; the rest of the town—eight or ten square blocks of it—was spread out to the south under the inevitable water tower. The buildings were all old, many of them Span-

ish-style; among them was one of those all-but-extinct Texaco
stations made of white stucco, with an arched, tile-edged por-
tico built out over hand-crank pumps. I passed a railroad yard,
a farm-equipment company, an auto body shop, a liquor store,
a market. Next in line was a café that in its front window
advertised Mexican food and barbecue. Hunger made me pull
over in front of the café; I hadn't bothered to eat breakfast this
morning.

I had the place to myself while I tucked away a bowl of
pretty good chili. I had my thoughts to myself, too, and I kept
wondering if I hadn't made a mistake in agreeing to help Arlo
Haas. And an even larger mistake in accepting the key to his
daughter's apartment that he'd insisted on giving me. It was
not the kind of investigation most private detectives would
take on, and rightly so. Too many unknown factors; too many
personal angles. But hell, I was a sucker for this kind of thing.
Now more than ever. That was something that hadn't been
changed by the three months I'd spent chained to the cabin
wall, the victim of a madman's warped desire for revenge. I'd
lost things during that time of suffering and its immediate
aftermath: patience, certain ethics, a kind of innocence. And
I'd gained things, too: the capacity for sudden anger and sudden violence, an impulsive recklessness, the sporadic fear of
being alone. I was a different man; there was no question of
that.

And yet in certain fundamental ways I was still the same
man. I still had compassion, sentimentality, the desire to right
wrongs and create order out of chaos; I was still the original
bleeding heart, a minor-league champion of the oppressed. If
I'd lost those qualities along with the other good ones, or if
they had been corrupted in any significant way, I could not
have continued to function as a detective or as a human being.
There would have been nothing left for me to live for, and
before very long the madman would have had his revenge after
all.

* * *

THE SAN BERNADO UNION SCHOOL was easy enough
to find. It was a block off the main drag, at the western end of
the town's residential area. Here, the Depression-era atmosphere was even more pronounced. The streets were either
partially paved or of unpaved gravel. Most of the houses had
been standing when I was born; were set back under tall cot-
tonwoods or droopy willows, or behind fences along which
cactus grew in thick clumps. Their yards had dusty grape ar-
bors, their porches rusty swings and discarded iceboxes and
clutches of moldering Sears, Roebuck furniture.

The school was relatively new at age thirty or so—a low,
beige cinder-block building, with two short wings that made it
into a stubby, squared-off U. Behind it was a weedy football
field, cracked asphalt tennis and basketball courts, a public
swimming pool. Parked in front were two lines of vehicles,
mostly pickups piloted by women waiting for their kids. Some
of the pickups had horse-trailers attached to them. Life in the
country. It was a shrinking way of life, though, narrowing
down to pockets like San Bernado. In the not too distant future, if the developers and the technocrats and the hucksters
had their way, the San Bernados would disappear, too, and the
customs and conventions of rural folk would become nothing
more than quaint historical curiosities . . . and then not even
that. Then they would be as forgotten as the man who invented buggy whips, as the conveyances he invented them for.

I found a place to park, went inside the school's main
entrance. The halls were empty; it was fifteen minutes shy of
two o'clock and classes were still in session. I followed an
arrow that said OFFICE and learned from a lady in gray that
Mary Ellen Crowley taught grades one through six and that
her homeroom was number eleven, in the south wing. The
gray lady said it would be all right for me to go there and talk
to her, but not until her last class let out at two.

I didn't want to go immediately to the south wing and
hang around in the hall; it would have made me feel like a
dirty old man. So I waited in the office instead. Finally a bell

rang and little piping voices and thundering feet rose to a
crescendo in the halls. When the stampede ended, I ventured
forth. There were still some kids loitering at rows of lockers; a
couple of them gave me wary looks as I passed, which made
me feel like a dirty old man anyway. Some days, you just can't
feel good about yourself no matter what you do.

Mary Ellen Crowley turned out to be a plump blonde with
attractive features, which she spoiled with too much eye-
shadow and plum-colored lipstick. She was smiling and
friendly until I showed her the Photostat of my investigator's
license and told her why I was there; then her manner turned
grave. But she was willing to talk about Grady Haas. She sat
behind her somewhat cluttered desk, and since there was no
place else I perched on one of the kids' desks. That didn't do
much for my self-esteem either.

"I'm worried about Grady too," she said. "Something's
badly wrong in her life, her dad's right about that."

"Did she give you any idea of what it is?"

"No. She didn't have much to say, didn't seem to want my
company. I didn't stay long."

"Are you and she still close friends?"

"I wouldn't say close, no. We've never been close."

"You keep in touch regularly?"

"Oh, we talk on the phone every few months."

"Letters?"

"No. Neither of us is a letter writer."

"Does Grady confide in you?"

"About her personal life? Not really. We've never shared
secrets, never talked about anything intimate that I can remember. She's a very hard person to get close to."

"And she's always been like that?"

"More or less."

"How would you characterize her?" I asked. "Is she withdrawn because she's shy or what?"

"Well, she's not exactly shy; just an extremely private person. I guess you could call her a dreamer."

"In what sense?"

"Not the romantic kind—you know, knights in shining armor and all that. She has an idealized version of the way things should be, and the real world doesn't measure up. Neither do people, even the ones she cares about. So for the most part she shuns the real world and lives according to her own ideals."

"That's a lonely way to live."

"I know. But that's how Grady wants it." Ms. Crowley paused thoughtfully. "I think her mother dying had a lot to do with the way she is now. And her father's stroke, too, later on."

"How do you mean?"

"Her parents were and are important to her. She wanted them to go on as they'd always been—strong, healthy, there for her when she needed them. When her mother died, it had a profound effect on her."

"Made her dislike and distrust the real world even more?"

"Yes."

"When did that happen?"

"Sixteen . . . no, seventeen years ago. We were juniors in high school."

"Cancer, wasn't it?"

"Breast cancer. Mrs. Haas was sick about six months. Grady took it even harder than her dad did. That's the real reason she left the valley right after graduation. She didn't even stay the summer before moving to the city and entering college."

"Was there any particular reason she picked U.S.F.?"

"Well, her family is Catholic."

"Aside from that. Why San Francisco? Why not a school in a smaller town?"

"She preferred the city. She never did like living here in the valley."

"Why, as private as she is?"

"It's easier to be alone in a big city than it is in the country," Ms. Crowley said. "Don't you think so?"

I thought so—and that it was a perceptive insight into Grady Haas. In an urban environment, if you choose, you don't have to deal with people except in glancing ways; you can wall yourself off, become a faceless entity in crowds of faceless entities. In the country, especially a little farm community like San Bernado where everybody knows everybody else's business, you can avoid neither contact nor scrutiny. It's like living in a house made of glass.

I asked, "Have you visited her in San Francisco?"

"We've had lunch a few times. And a couple of years ago, when my car broke down while I was in the city, I spent the night at her apartment."

"Did you meet any of her friends on those occasions?"

"I doubt if Grady has any friends up there."

"She's never mentioned anyone to you?"

"Just one person. A man she was seeing last year."

"Ted or Todd something? Her father couldn't remember."

"Todd Bellin."

"B-e-l-l-i-n?"

"I don't know, I never saw it written out."

"How long was she involved with him?"

"Three or four months, I think."

"And then they broke up."

"Around Thanksgiving."

"Did Grady tell you why?"

"He asked her to marry him and she said no."

"Why did she turn him down?"

"She wasn't ready to make a commitment, she said."

"Meaning she wasn't ready to let anyone share her life?"

"That's what it amounted to," Ms. Crowley said, nodding. "Being married not only means living with someone, it means sharing yourself with that person every day. You can't live inside yourself when you're married, and I guess Grady realized that. Of course, if Todd Bellin had been her ideal man

. . . well, then her answer might have been different. But obviously he wasn't."

"What is her ideal man?"

"She'd never say. But every woman has one, just as every man has an ideal woman."

"How did Bellin take her rejection?"

"She wouldn't discuss it."

"Did you feel there might have been bitter feelings on his part?"

Ms. Crowley considered that. In the silence, a kid's voice yelled suddenly outside the windows, "You stupid shit! You do that again and I'll kill you!"

Well, that was one thing that had already changed in the country, one of the little corruptions of modern society: aggression, public and obscene, and so prevalent that even little kids picked it up. But it wasn't the only change, not by a damn sight. Drugs, AIDS, unrepentant greed, casual violence—those and a dozen others, simmering just under the surface of this and a thousand other little American towns. San Bernado wasn't frozen in the past; it just looked that way. Its metamorphosis was under way, insidiously, and it wouldn't be long at all before it emerged into the new century. Reality check; pay attention now. The past is dead and gone. And the present is barely controlled chaos under a thin veneer of high-tech civilization. And the future . . . the future scared the hell out of me.

Ms. Crowley's voice intruded. I shook my head and said, "I'm sorry, I didn't catch that. I was woolgathering."

"I said that when Grady came home last Christmas, she seemed even more withdrawn than usual. I don't know if that had anything to do with Todd Bellin, but I suspected at the time that it might."

"Did she mention his name then?"

"No."

"Do you have any idea where he lives?"

"In the city, I think. But not where."

"Or what he does for a living?"

"I'm not sure. He may work in a bank."

"What gave you that impression?"

"I remember Grady telling me she met him in a bank. Of course, that might mean they were both customers, but she also said he kept asking her out every time she saw him and finally she surprised herself by saying yes. I took that to mean every time she saw him at the bank."

"Which bank does she use, do you know?"

"No, I don't."

"Did she tell you anything at all about Bellin? What kind of man he is, good and bad qualities?"

"Nothing like that, no. Just that they liked the same things —you know, music and films and types of food. And that she felt bad about turning him down. He doesn't sound like someone who would become violently angry over a rejection."

"No, he doesn't," I said.

"Besides," Ms. Crowley said, "it's been six months since they broke up. I don't see how Todd Bellin could have anything to do with Grady's trouble now."

I had a thought about that, but I did not put it into words. It was possible Bellin was an unstable personality and had spent those six months nursing a grudge. Left Grady alone, or mostly alone, until the grudge festered to the point where he'd lost control and started hassling her—made threats, maybe embarked on a little campaign of terror. The love-turned-to-hate syndrome. That kind of thing happened too often in these days of open aggression, casual violence, and people living too close to the edge.

You stupid shit! You hurt me again and I'll kill you!

Yet Arlo Haas had said that Grady was "busted up inside and in shock," but no longer afraid; resigned, as if "she don't care anymore." You can go into shock when your life is threatened, but then it wears off and fear takes firmer root. With Grady it seemed to be the other way around. What could a rejected suitor do to you that would cause that kind of reaction? What could *anybody* do to you?

All right, enough of that. I was getting ahead of myself, playing worst-case scenario, and that was not good detective work. The fact was, I had too few facts to indulge in any worthwhile speculating. Different things hurt different people in different ways, and some of them have no more substance than phantoms at high noon. With any luck that was all we were dealing with here—phantoms at high noon.

Chapter 3

IT WAS ALMOST SIX by the time I got back to San Francisco, thanks to commuter-traffic snarls on both ends of San Jose. And it was just shy of six-thirty when I finished inching my way across town to O'Farrell Street. The old building near Van Ness that houses the agency offices was locked up tight. Eberhardt never stays after four-thirty, except in cases of dire emergency, and these days he was too immersed in his wedding mania to do much work anyway; and the other two businesses that occupy the premises—Bay City Realtors, on the first floor, and the Slim-Taper Shirt Company, "The Slim-Taper Look Is the Right Look," on the second floor—both shut down operations promptly at five-thirty. I unlocked the street door, rode the casket-sized elevator up to the top floor, and let myself into the converted loft that was my home away from home.

Two messages on the answering machine, neither important. On my desk, a note from Eberhardt in his near-illegible scrawl that I deciphered as: *Don't forget to pick up your tux. Hinkle will have ready 8 A.M. tomorrow.*

I sighed. These past couple of weeks Eb had become a royal pain in the ass. A man who was about to be married for the second time at the age of fifty-eight was entitled to a certain amount of prenuptial frenzy, but he had far exceeded his allotment. What had started out as a simple affair—civil ceremony with Kerry and me as witnesses, a few friends to his house for a wedding buffet afterward—he had manipulated into an elaborate church wedding with a guest list of more than sixty and a catered reception that required the renting of a hall. And a five-day honeymoon in La Jolla had since become a ten-day honeymoon on Waikiki. This was all his doing; Bobbie Jean Addison, his somewhat shy and beleaguered bride-to-be, had been caught up in and swamped by the tide of his lunacy.

This business of tuxedos was his latest aberration. It wouldn't do, he'd decided a few days ago, for the two of them to get married in ordinary clothing. Oh no, Bobbie Jean and Kerry had to wear gowns and he and I had to wear soup-and-fish. Bobbie Jean argued with him. I argued with him even more vehemently. The last time I'd worn a rented tuxedo, on a job over in Ross that I did not like to remember, I'd split the crotch out of the damn pants climbing through a window—an episode that had cost me my thirty-buck deposit and a priceless amount of humiliation. The thought of donning a monkey suit again made me itch. But Eberhardt wouldn't listen to reason. It was gowns and tuxedos and that, by God, was that.

Five days to go, I told myself. Just five more days, and the two of them will be on their blissful way to Hawaii and things will get back to normal around here.

But five days is a long time. An eternity when you're dealing with a crazy man. What else he might think up between now and Saturday afternoon was the stuff of bad dreams and Abbott and Costello movies.

At the Haas farm I'd had Arlo Haas sign a standard agency contract and give me a check to cover two days' work; I filed the contract and put the check in the lockbox in my desk, for deposit later. Then I threw Eberhardt's note in the wastebasket and closed the office again and went home to spend a quiet evening by myself.

Or so I thought until I got there.

I HEARD THE MUSIC as I came down the hall to the door of my flat. Jazz, the soft moody kind; Miles Davis. Ah, I thought. I keyed open the door. All the lights were on and the jazz was coming from one of my albums playing on the stereo. And Kerry was sitting on the couch, barefoot, her legs tucked under her, snugly wrapped in a tatty bathrobe of mine—the blue chenille one I used to wear when I was forty pounds heavier than I am now.

Her hair was down, combed out long over shoulders, the lampglow giving it deep-burgundy highlights. She was not beautiful in any classic sense; some men, the kind who equate beauty with paint and plastic and clonelike perfection—one of the Stepford wives, for instance—might even have called her plain. But to me she was the most beautiful woman I'd ever known. Just looking at her made me ache inside. It wasn't all physical either. I had an emotional attachment to Kerry Wade that was sometimes a little unnerving in its intensity. Without her I could not have survived the first few months after I came home from my mountain ordeal. Without her I'm not sure I could go on very long even now.

"Well, it's about time," she said as I shut the door.

"Hiya, toots."

"Toots," she said and rolled her eyes. At her elbow, I saw then, was a glass of wine. On her lap was a pulp magazine from my collection, one of the later issues of *Black Mask,* the cover of which depicted a half-naked Hollywood starlet in a fur-trimmed cape who was attempting to brain a gun-toting mug with an Oscar statuette. Just another day in La-La Land. "You sound like the detective in the story I've been reading."

"All private eyes have to sound like pulp detectives once in a while. It's in our union contracts."

"Hah," she said. "I was beginning to think you weren't coming home tonight. Where were you?"

"In the Salinas Valley on a case."

"New case?"

"Yup. I'll tell you about it later." I shrugged out of my overcoat, threw it over the back of a chair, moved around to where I could see her better. "I'd have managed to get here a lot sooner if I'd known you'd be waiting. Why didn't you tell me you could get away tonight?"

"I didn't know until this afternoon. A couple of people from Children of Grieving Parents went to see Cybil, and she actually let them talk her into attending an open house at a Marin seniors' complex. They won't have her back until at least ten."

"Now that is good news. On both counts."

"I thought you'd be pleased. Have you eaten?"

"No."

"Good. I made dinner for us."

"Such domesticity. What are we having?"

"You'll see . . . later." She stretched lazily, like a cat. The hem of the robe fell away and revealed most of one slim, bare leg. "Aren't you going to kiss me?" she said.

I went over and leaned down and gave her a short one. That wasn't good enough for her. She caught hold of my ears, both of them, and yanked my head down and bruised my mouth a little, wetly. When she finally let go she licked her own mouth, again like a cat, and favored me with a sloe-eyed look.

"Wanna get laid, big boy?"

"Gee," I said, "I don't know. I'm hungry and kind of tired. . . ."

"What *I* am is horny. It's been eight days."

"You keep track, huh?"

"Damn right. Well?"

"Suppose I'm not in the mood?"

"You Italians are *always* in the mood."

"You think so? Maybe you don't know me as well as you think you do."

"Want to bet?" she said.

Smiling, she stood up, taking her time about it. She loosened the belt at her waist and shrugged out of the robe, taking her time about that too. Then she struck a pose, with one hand on a provocatively arched hip.

I said, staring, "You're naked."

"Such powers of observation! Such ratiocination! Shall we?"

"We shall."

And we did.

DINNER, WHEN WE GOT AROUND TO IT, was a spinach salad and chicken parmigiana. While we ate we talked some more about Kerry's seventy-five-year-old mother, Cybil Wade—a too-frequent topic of conversation these past several months. But it wasn't half as bleak a subject now as it had been.

Cybil had been Kerry's roommate since December, a few weeks after Kerry's father, Ivan, died suddenly of a heart attack. All her life Cybil had been strong and self-sufficient, but Ivan's death had had a crippling effect on her. It left her unable to cope with her loss or with the prospect of living out her remaining time alone; she had a horror of being shut away in a nursing home, of dying in such a place. So she'd put her L.A. house up for sale, talked Kerry into letting her move in, and virtually retreated from both society and reality.

Her depression and smothering dependency had been hard enough on Kerry; two factors made it even worse. One was that Cybil had turned against me, an irrational reaction to the active dislike Ivan and I had felt for each other. For more than four months now it had been impossible for me to visit Kerry at home, and difficult for us to spend much time together. The other factor was that Kerry's building in Diamond Heights was in the process of going condo. Kerry wasn't sure at first that she could afford the asking price; she was afraid she'd have to find a new place to rent and then move not only herself but Cybil as well.

Things finally began to ease a bit when Kerry joined Children of Grieving Parents, a support group that helped her deal with her mother's problems and was now helping Cybil do the same. They'd eased even more when she'd been able to arrange a bank loan that would allow her to buy her apartment. Cybil's progress had been slow, but the fact that she was letting herself be trotted off to a seniors complex open-house was encouraging. That type of complex—private condos with available recreational facilities and a clinic staffed by medical personnel and counselors—was everyone's ultimate goal for her.

"If the place makes a favorable impression on Cybil," Kerry said, "she'll want to tell me all about it when she gets home tonight. Keep your fingers crossed."

"Yup."

"I'll give you a full report in the morning, either way." She sighed. "I love that woman dearly but Lord I hope she makes up her mind *soon*. I'm just too selfish to go on sharing my life with her at such close quarters."

"You're not selfish," I said, "you're emotionally taxed."

"Selfish, too, my love. We all are to one degree or another, particularly those of us who won't see forty again. It's not such a bad trait, you know. There's a big qualitative difference between being selfish and being self-centered."

"I know. Eberhardt taught me that."

"You think he's self-centered?"

"Don't you? Now?"

"Oh," she said, "the wedding."

"What else? All this fancy stuff is for his sake, not Bobbie Jean's. Just a big ego trip."

"Poor Bobbie Jean," Kerry said. "She's at her wits' end."

"You talk to her today?"

"Last night. She called about the white-gown nonsense."

"What white-gown nonsense?"

"Didn't Eb tell you?"

"No. I haven't seen him since Saturday."

"Well, now he wants Bobbie Jean to wear white."

"Why, for God's sake?"

"He's got some silly idea that brides should always wear white. Even when they're fifty-one, have been married twice before, and have two grown daughters."

"Is she going along with it?"

"No, she put her foot down this time. She already has her wedding dress and she's not about to pay for another. She's had all the plan-changing she can stand."

"Me, too, with his damn tuxedos," I said. "One more crazy idea and I swear I'll strangle him with his own cummerbund."

It was nearing nine-thirty by the time we finished eating, and Kerry said she'd better scoot. I told her I'd take care of the dishes—but I didn't do them right away. Instead, I followed her into the bedroom and sat on the bed to watch her dress. There is almost as much erotic pleasure in watching a woman you love put her clothes on as there is in watching her take her clothes off.

She was zipping up her skirt when she made a sudden giggling sound, as if she'd just been tickled or goosed. "I heard a good joke today," she said.

"Dirty joke?"

"Mildly bawdy. Want to hear it?"

"Boy," I said. "Steamy sex, a home-cooked meal, and now a racy joke. What more could a man want of an evening?"

She wrinkled her nose at me. "I know you're not big on jokes, but this one is funny. One of our clients"—she was a senior copywriter at the Bates and Carpenter ad agency—"told it at lunch."

"Some client. Did he also leer suggestively and pat your fanny?"

"Her name is Rebecca Kiefer and she's the chief honcho at KSUN radio."

"Oh," I said.

"You want to hear the joke or don't you?"

"I want to hear it."

"All right. After a long hard day at the office, this attractive career woman—a person not unlike myself—decides to stop in at a small cocktail lounge for a drink to relax her before going home. Unfortunately, the lounge happens to be occupied by one of those handsome macho types who think they're God's gift and no woman could possibly refuse their charms. He sits down at her table, uninvited, introduces himself as Doug, and proceeds to tell her what a truly wonderful lover he is—how a night of passion with him is an experience to be treasured for years afterward. He's so sure of himself that he segues into the subject of sexual positions without missing a beat. Not only has he tried every one in the *Kama Sutra,* he says, he's invented a couple of new ones himself.

"Before he can tell her just what they are, the career woman gives him an innocent smile and says, 'That's all very well and good, Doug, but I couldn't do anything really kinky with a man I hardly know. I'm the old-fashioned type. The only way for a woman like me and a man like you is the jungle missionary position.'

" 'The jungle missionary position?' he says. 'Is that the same as the standard missionary position?'

" 'Oh no,' she says. 'Here's how it works. I go home and take a long luxuriant bath in warm water scented with different exotic oils. Then I dry off and anoint my body with powder and perfume. Then I put primitive music on the CD player, the kind that's full of drums and animal grunts and pagan cries. Then I get into bed—naked, of course—and arrange myself comfortably on my back. And while I'm doing all of that . . .' She pauses, drawing out the moment.

"By this time Doug's tongue is hanging out. He says, 'Yeah? While you're doing all of that, what do I do?'

"And she says, 'You join a religious sect, fly to Africa, get lost in the jungle, and are never heard from again.' "

I WAS STILL CHUCKLING when Kerry left ten minutes later.

Chapter **4**

THE UNIVERSITY OF SAN FRANCISCO is the city's oldest institution of higher learning, having been founded by a Jesuit priest in 1855. Its first campus was completely destroyed by fire in the 1906 quake; the present campus was built a few years later atop the hill at Fulton and Parker, above the eastern edge of Golden Gate Park. For most of its existence the university was strictly the dominion of Catholic males; women weren't allowed in until the early sixties. Once U.S.F. turned coeducational, though, it made the transition intelligently and with dispatch. Now it graduates as many women as men, and has a very good School of Nursing to go with its School of Law and its above-average colleges of Liberal Arts, Science, and Business Administration.

Its main campus sprawls over twenty-odd acres; a few blocks away, atop a much smaller hill, is its newer Lone Mountain campus. The neighborhood that surrounds the two is residential—older middle-class homes and small apartment buildings that serve chiefly as off-campus housing for students. Temescal Terrace runs between the main campus and the uni-

versity's soccer field, one of several block-long streets that fill
the gap. There was only one apartment building among the
private homes standing shoulder to shoulder along its length:
three floors, three units, and like its neighbors, Spanish in style
—beige stucco with blue trim and a blue tile roof. It was set
back from the sidewalk just far enough to permit a couple of
yucca trees to maintain a root-hold.

All of the available street parking was taken when I came
cruising along at nine on Tuesday morning, so I had to leave
my car around the corner on Turk. The day was bright, clear,
cold—a good day to be out and about in the city. Unless you
were on your way to invade someone's home, someone who
valued her privacy above all else. Yes, it was part of the job I'd
been hired to do; yes, I had her father's permission and a key
to go with it; yes, it was with the best of intentions. But the
justifications didn't make me feel any less like a sneak.

Her apartment was the bottommost of the three, the one
with its fronting windows tightly draped against prying eyes.
The first mailbox in the narrow vestibule bore her name and
was jammed full, as I could see by the view slot. No post-office
hold on her mail indicated that her leaving town had been
sudden and unplanned, which in turn suggested flight rather
than a simple urge to get away for a while.

The key Arlo Haas had given me opened the building door
as well. Inside was a bare tile-floored lobby and a staircase and
a heavy blue door with the numeral *1* on it. The building was
without audible sound; so was Grady's apartment when I laid
my ear against the door. I rang the bell anyway. Haas had said
she lived alone, but I did not want to take the chance of walking in on anybody. I thumbed the button twice more before I
was ready to use the key.

The interior was dusky, with just a little natural light out-
lining the drawn front drapes and another wedge of it coming
through a doorway opposite the window. In the air was a faint,
spicy-sweet smell—potpourri. My mother kept the stuff
around and it was a childhood scent I'd never forgotten. I shut

the door, felt along the wall until I located a light switch. It lit up two lamps, one on an end table and the other atop a writing desk. I stood looking around, getting a feel of the place.

The living room was tastefully furnished, though in a style that didn't appeal to me. White wicker and light maplewood furniture. Wallpaper and drapery in little flower patterns. Some hanging ferns in wicker baskets; a couple of other plants, already in need of water and sunlight, on wicker stands. A big pottery bowl full of the potpourri. An even bigger stuffed toy duck, patterned in the same fabric as the drapery, with a fluffy bow tied around its neck. All done in pink and light blues and dominant white. Everything arranged just so, in such harmonious accord that I wondered if she'd had a decorator do it. Probably not; from what I'd learned about her so far, she was not the decorator type.

The carpet was white pile, very clean. It made me want to check my back trail for dirty footprints as I crossed it. In the dining area the floor was bare parquet, partially covered by a rag rug in pinks and blues. Maplewood table and chairs, maple breakfront with a display of old-fashioned flower-patterned plates on bent-wire stands. Nothing else.

Kitchen. A smaller rag rug on the floor. Pottery bowls, copper pots, decorative baskets, two more hanging ferns. The sink and all the fixtures gleamed as brightly as if they had been polished with some kind of shine-enhancer.

Bathroom. Still another rag rug, a hanging fuschia. And the same gleam on the fixtures. Even the shelves inside the medicine cabinet sparkled, the items on them set in precise rows.

Bedroom, the last of the apartment's rooms. Window edged with frilly white curtains and overlooking a small rear garden. Brass bed with an organdy spread and throw pillows trimmed in lace, cherrywood rocker, cherrywood cabinet hiding the blind eye of a TV set, matching dresser and nightstands. A low brass bookcase sat next to an open mirror-doored closet, the topmost of its shelves filled with a set of

books in red leatherette bindings—the complete works of
Steinbeck. The other two shelves held paperbacks and a few
hardcovers, all of which were either historical fiction or biog-
raphies of historical figures. Like me, Grady Haas seemed
more comfortable with the past than with the present or future.

Arranged on the dresser were another bowl of potpourri, a
white satin jewelry box, and a few assorted perfume and co-
logne bottles. On one of the nightstands was a hardcover book
—John Jakes's *California Gold*—from which protruded a fat
cardboard bookmark shaped like a duck; on the other nightstand were two ornately framed photographs, one of her father
and the other of a thin, dark woman I recognized from the
photos in her father's house. Her mother.

On the way back to the living room I thought: Somebody's
been here since she left. Somebody else who doesn't belong.

It was not any one thing; it was the cumulative effect
of several little things. Grady Haas was a meticulous housekeeper, and meticulous in her personal habits as well. A place
for everything and everything in its place. Except that everything *wasn't* in its place. That could have been the result of
haste in quitting here last Friday, but I didn't think so. Meticulous people are meticulous even in times of hurry and stress;
it's an automatic response with them. She would not have
taken the time to pack a bag, as she had obviously done, and
then gone away leaving her home in its present state.

In the living room papers were strewn over the surface of
the maple writing desk; a few others were on the floor underneath. Two of the desk drawers were open a few inches. A
drawer was open in the breakfront in the dining area, and so
were drawers in one of the bedroom nightstands and the
dresser. Inside the bedroom closet, a storage box that had been
lifted off an upper shelf sat on the floor, its lid off, its contents
disarranged. The clincher was the photographs of her mother
and father. Both had been lying flat instead of upright, and the
cardboard backs were loose in the frames—worked free to see

if anything was hidden there or if there was writing on the backs of the photos.

Somebody hunting for something, I thought. A room-by-room search by a person who had his emotions under control but who didn't really care if Grady came back and realized he'd been there.

Why? Looking for what?

I scanned through the papers on the desk. This year's paid bills, receipts, cancelled checks. No personal correspondence of any kind. I inventoried each of the drawers without finding anything of interest—and without finding either a Rolodex or an address book, even though the desk was where she kept her telephone. The searcher might have taken one or the other. More likely, there hadn't been one to take. A person who has no friends, who shuns social activities, would keep in her head or in a little book in her purse what few addresses and telephone numbers she needed.

I searched the rest of the room, even going so far as to lift cushions and get down on all fours to probe under furniture. Nothing. Nothing for me, either, in the dining area or kitchen. The storage box in the bedroom closet was filled with older papers, envelopes containing Grady's income-tax records for the past two years, and a packet of Christmas and birthday cards tied with a pink ribbon. All but two of the cards were signed "Your Dad" and "Love, Mary Ellen"; the other two— one birthday, one Christmas—bore the words "With everything good and sweet, always, Todd" in a careful hand. Apparently Grady had a small sentimental streak. And yet, I'd seen nothing else here that linked her to her roots in the Salinas Valley. No other photos, no school yearbooks, no childhood mementoes. If she'd kept any such things, they were probably still in San Bernado; she had limited space here. Or was the reason that she shunned reminders of a youth that was painful to her?

The remainder of the closet was in order, except that a few of the articles of clothing on hangers were rumpled, as if the searcher had been feeling through pockets. Grady's taste in clothes matched her taste in interior design: prints and pastels, mostly, with a few plain whites mixed in. The dresser held no revelations; neither did the nightstand on which the photographs lay. The drawer in the other nightstand contained a half-empty package of Trojan condoms. The condoms surprised me a little, more than they should have. Hell, she was thirty-one years old; did I expect her to be a virgin just because she lived a solitary life and preferred the past to the present? I examined the package, but there was no way of telling how long ago it had been bought. Back when she was dating Todd Bellin, maybe. Or last month or last week.

Frustrated, I returned to the living room. There was nothing here to explain Grady's run home, or why someone had come to search the apartment. Or to indicate if the searcher had found whatever it was he was looking for. Or to tell me if Grady had taken something with her when she left.

I poked my head out into the lobby; still empty, the building still quiet. Then I got down on one knee to examine the locking mechanism on the door. It was a deadbolt, which meant that forcing it would have required effort and would have left telltale marks. There were no marks. The searcher had to have a key, then. Given to him by Grady, recently or sometime in the past? Stolen from her?

I set the deadbolt, went out into the lobby and closed the door and tested it to make sure it was locked. Behind the staircase, I noticed then, was an unmarked door that I hadn't seen on the way in. Grady's apartment key opened that one too. More stairs, this set leading into the basement. I found a light switch and descended.

Musty and gloomy, like all basements, it was concretefloored. At the back end, another door led into the garden. Against the wall opposite the stairs, three screened and gated storage cages held the tenants' larger personal belongings.

Each of the cages was numbered and padlocked. But the padlock on number one wouldn't keep anybody out. One of its staples had been neatly sawn through with a hacksaw blade, then set back in place through its hasp. You had to step up close to see the damage.

There was not much inside. A Schwinn bicycle, a large leather suitcase that looked to be part of a set, two extra chairs and a table leaf for Grady's dining room set, a folding cot that had been bought new and seldom used since. And half a dozen storage cartons, the tops open or loosely closed on all of them, the contents pawed through. One contained more old files dating back several years, another softcover books, a third extra bedding, a fourth dishes, a fifth pots and pans, and the sixth figurines and pewter items and other gewgaws that had once been carefully wrapped in tissue. The box of files had received the most thorough going-over. But if there'd been anything to find, the searcher had made off with it.

I replaced the sawn padlock on the cage door, went back up into the lobby. I had an urge to search Grady's apartment again, but it was an urge born of frustration and I didn't give in to it. Instead I walked out into the vestibule and looked at the names on the other two mailboxes.

The second-floor apartment was occupied by M. Norman and C. Tagliozzi; the third-floor tenant, or tenants, was named Voorhees. Maybe one of them could tell me something. But when I rang first one bell and then the other, I got no response. I'd been alone in the building the whole time.

Chapter **5**

THE OFFICE WAS locked up tight, the steam heat still turned off: Eberhardt hadn't put in an appearance yet, even though it was past ten-thirty. He was a chronic latecomer, and since his wedding madness he'd been even more erratic. The backlog of work on his desk had grown to alarming proportions; I would have to farm some of it out while he was away on his fancy Hawaiian honeymoon.

Irritated, I put the heat on and made coffee and checked for messages. Then I called Arlo Haas. He said things were the same there. I asked him where Grady did her banking. Bank of America, he said, just as she always had, but he wasn't sure which branch. He could find out quickly, though; she'd already gone off into the hills and she hadn't taken her purse with her.

He called back within fifteen minutes. Her bank was the Kearney Street branch, in the Financial District, near where Intercoastal Insurance had its offices. Haas wanted to know if I was getting anywhere yet, if I'd gone to her apartment—asking the questions reluctantly, as though he didn't want to be pushy, but asking them anyway because he couldn't restrain himself. I told him, gently, that I'd contact him as soon as I had any information to relate. To his credit, he let it go at that.

I got B of A's Kearney Street branch number out of the directory. The woman who answered my call sounded young and out of breath, as if she'd had to run a long distance to get to the phone. I said, "Good morning. Can you tell me, please, if you have a Mr. Todd Bellin employed there?"

"Yes. Yes we do."

"In what capacity?"

"He's one of our tellers. But he isn't in today."

"Oh? How come?"

"The flu or something. He didn't come in yesterday either. May I take a message?"

I told her no, no message, and rang off. So Bellin was off work this week too. Coincidence? Or was there some connection between his absence and Grady's sudden flight?

I looked up Bellin's name in the directory. He was listed; the address was Twenty-first Street, and from the number, I judged the location to be at the southern edge of the Mission District, only a couple of miles from here. I was making a note of the address, and of the telephone number in case I needed it, when Eberhardt blew in.

He wore a half-frazzled, half-preoccupied expression, and his appearance was even more rumpled than usual. His suit needed pressing, his shirt needed washing, his tie needed to go to Goodwill. He'd given himself a patchy shave this morning, missing an entire little thicket of stubble on the left side of his jaw. And he'd only combed about three-quarters of his hair; a hunk of it stood straight up in back, flapping when he moved like a tattered gray pennant.

"Somebody break your alarm clock?" I asked him.

"Don't start in on me. I got a lot of things on my mind."

"None of which have to do with work."

"I said don't start on me. You pick up your tux yet?"

"Now *you're* starting on *me.*"

"Did you or didn't you?"

"Not yet. I'll get it before I go home tonight."

He grunted something unintelligible and went to pour himself some of the coffee I'd made. Then he said, "Rehearsal, Friday night at the church. Eight sharp. For Chrissake don't forget."

"Eb, will you ease off a little? Give yourself a break, and the rest of us too."

"I don't know what you're talking about."

"The hell you don't."

"You think a wedding like this just happens by itself? Somebody's got to make sure everything gets done."

"Sure. But not by badgering people and changing details at the last minute. You've changed your mind more often than you change your underwear."

"Very funny. See how hard I'm laughing?"

"It's the truth, my friend, and you know it."

He didn't have an answer for that. But he was glowering as he moved to his desk, and when he sat down he did it agitatedly enough to slosh coffee over some of the papers littering its top. He muttered something angry and turned the glower on me.

"See what you made me do?" he said.

I laughed at him. He didn't like that, but he didn't say anything about it. He pretended to be busy mopping up the coffee spill with his handkerchief.

The mood I was in, I felt like needling him a little. I said, "What color tuxes did you order?"

"Black. Red tie, red cummerbund."

"You sure that's what you want?"

"Sure I'm sure. Why?"

"Well, I thought maybe you'd prefer white. To match the gown you tried to get Bobbie Jean to wear."

Dark silence. Then, "She tell you about that?"

"Doesn't matter who told me. Dumb ideas get around fast."

"It's not a dumb idea. Brides are supposed to wear white."

"Virgin brides."

"Virgins don't have a monopoly on white," he said defensively. "You sound like Bobbie Jean. A suggestion, that's all it was, and you two make a federal case out of it."

"You got any other brilliant suggestions lurking in that fertile brain of yours?"

"Just one," he said. "How about you stick your head up your ass and whistle 'Yankee Doodle'?"

"You know what I like most about you, Eb? Your dignity. Even when the heat's on, you're a paragon of poise, erudition, and devastating wit."

"Fuck you," he said.

I laughed at him so hard this time he got up, stormed out of the office, and slammed the door behind him.

TODD BELLIN'S ADDRESS turned out to be one of two flats in an old wood-frame building half a block off Potrero Avenue, directly opposite San Francisco General Hospital. Fringe of the Mission, all right—a downscale, mixed-bag neighborhood dominated by Latins, with a sprinkling of Lebanese and Asian merchants and a spray of Anglo pensioners, old-line blue-collar families, and low-salaried young couples and singles. Some of the more solid Victorians in the area had been refurbished and attractively repainted; too many of the other structures were being allowed to decay. Bellin's was one of the latter, though not so long ago some misguided soul had attempted to spruce up its sagging facade with a coat of paint. The effect—a sort of pink with turd-brown trim—was the same as if you slapped too much rouge and mascara on a doddery harridan: an embarrassment and an eyesore.

I parked among some wind-gathered litter across the street and went over into its narrow vestibule. There were no mailboxes; each of the two doors had a mail slot cut in it and a different street number painted above. From the arrangement of the doors I judged that Bellin's was the upstairs flat, the one with both its fronting windows blinded by heavy muslin drapes. I prodded the bell button alongside his door, setting off a defective set of chimes—one squeaky discordant note in the middle and another at the end.

The door stayed shut. After thirty seconds I rang the squeaky chimes a second time; waited another thirty seconds and tried once more. Nobody home. Which didn't have to mean anything significant. Maybe he was just playing hooky from his job this week; people do that all the time. Even me, every now and then.

I turned out of the vestibule, started across the street. And as I did I happened to glance back at the building, the way you do—just in time to see a pale face peering out between a slit in one set of drapes upstairs. An instant later the face was gone and the drapes were tightly joined again.

I got into my car, thinking: So he's home after all. Just not dealing with visitors . . . or maybe it's strangers he's not dealing with.

Well?

THE SAN FRANCISCO OFFICES of Intercoastal Insurance were housed on four floors of a newish high-rise on Kearney Street. Their damage claims department, according to the lobby directory, was located on the lowest of the four. An ultrafast elevator disgorged me into a Spartan reception area— four chairs, one table, one asymmetrical desk with telephone intercom system, one receptionist—done up in shimmery pale-green hues that made me feel as though I had stepped into an underwater enclosure instead of one fifteen stories in the air. The receptionist spoiled the aquatic illusion, though. He was about twenty-two, had a face like a blond rhino without its horn, and lisped when he talked.

I gave him my name and one of my business cards and asked to see Lisa Fisher on a business matter concerning Grady Haas. Yes, I knew Ms. Haas was on vacation; it was Ms. Fisher I wanted to see. No, I didn't have an appointment.

Yes, it was a matter of some importance. He told me to have a
seat and he would see if Ms. Fisher was available. I had a seat.
Ms. Fisher was available, it turned out, but by the clock on
one wall eight minutes had passed before she appeared
through an inner door.

She was not much older than the lisping rhino; thin, pale,
with lusterless brown hair sitting astride her narrow skull in a
tidy pile. She wore granny glasses and a dark blue suit that
emphasized the angular planes of her body. When I handed
her another of my cards she stared at it for five seconds before
she said, with her lips pulled into a little moue, "Are you here
on company business?"

"No. As I told the receptionist, I'm here about Grady
Haas."

"I don't understand. What about Ms. Haas?"

"Would you mind if we talked in private?"

She made the moue again—it was her version of a frown—
but allowed as how she didn't mind. She led me through the
inner door, among an unquiet rabbit warren of modular cubi-
cles, and into a cubicle with her name on it. It didn't have a
window on the city; neither did the somewhat larger, empty
one adjoining it that I took to be Grady's. What it did have
was a functional green-metal desk, a computer terminal, one
desk chair with arms, one straight chair without arms, a functional green-metal file cabinet, and no more than four feet of
unoccupied space. It reminded me of a fluorescent-lit cell. This
was not a place you would want to work in if you suffered even
mildly from claustrophobia.

She sat in her desk chair, I sat on the straight chair, and
we looked at each other. Pretty soon she said, "About Ms.
Haas?" with a wary eagerness in her voice. Not quite as if she
were hoping for the worst; as if she were hoping for something
juicy that she could toss around among her coworkers later
on.

"Well, it's like this," I said confidentially. "I have information concerning an amount of money to which Ms. Haas may

be entitled. But I won't know for sure until I talk to her and complete my investigation."

"Oh," Ms. Fisher said. "You're an heir hunter, then?"

I wasn't surprised that she knew about heir hunters. That particular breed of sleuth has proliferated in recent years; they're known as "rag-pickers," among other things, because they wade through probate petitions filed with county clerks, looking for unpaid bequests and the words "heir—address unknown." Then they track down the heir, using all sorts of sources ranging from morticians and fraternal organizations to insurance companies, and arrange with the lucky individual for a cut of whatever they can wangle—up to forty percent, in some cases—as a finder's fee. The fact that Ms. Fisher was familiar with the heir-chasing game meant that she also had some idea of how they operated, and that in turn meant I would have to be even more careful in running my little ruse.

I said, "Well, not exactly. I don't specialize in locating missing heirs; it's one of several different types of investigative work that I do."

"I see. And you say Ms. Haas may be entitled to some money?" Behind her granny glasses, her pale blue eyes said she wasn't exactly tickled at the prospect.

"Yes, that's right."

"An inheritance from a deceased relative?"

"A deceased person who *may* have been her relative."

"Of course. How much of a bequest, may I ask?"

"I'm not at liberty to say."

"Well, is it a large amount?"

"Let's say it's substantial."

"You haven't told Ms. Haas yet?"

"No," I said. "That's why I'm here. I can't seem to pinpoint her current whereabouts."

"She's on vacation. Since last Friday."

"So I understand. Would you have any idea where she's gone?" That was a safe question: according to Arlo Haas, Ms. Fisher was unaware that Grady was in San Bernado.

"I'm sorry, I don't. She left . . . well, kind of suddenly."

"How do you mean?"

"She didn't give any advance notice that she intended to take vacation time. Last Thursday, I mean, the last time I saw her. She just called in on Friday." The moue reappeared; it made her look a little like a goldfish at feeding time. "It's a good thing we're not busy or I'd be swamped with work. It really wasn't very professional of her."

"No, it wasn't. Can you give me the name of anyone who might know where I can find her?"

"Well, there's her father. He called asking about her yesterday morning, as a matter of fact. But I don't know where he lives."

"Anyone here in the office?"

"I doubt that."

"A friend outside the office, someone you might know or she might have mentioned?"

"I don't know any of her friends. Ms. Haas . . . well, she's very closemouthed. She doesn't talk about her private life."

And you resent her for it, I thought. I said, "I understand she was involved with a man named Todd Bellin last year, an employee at her bank. Do you know him?"

"No."

"She never mentioned his name?"

"I'd remember if she had. Was it, um, a serious relationship?"

"I don't know. I haven't talked to Bellin yet either."

"I can't imagine Ms. Haas being serious about any man," she said, and stopped, and made the moue again. "Well, actually, maybe I can."

"How do you mean?"

"I think she may have met someone recently," Ms. Fisher said.

"Oh? But you don't know for sure?"

"No. Of course, she didn't talk about it."

"What makes you think she met someone?"

"The way she acted. That day after she came back to the office, I mean. Flustered . . . and she's *never* flustered. She had that look, too. You know, in her eyes. I know that look." Ms. Fisher said the last with a hint of jealousy, as if she'd never had the look herself and felt cheated when she observed it in others.

"How long ago was this?"

"Three weeks. April Fools' Day." The moue, followed by a chuckle with more than a dollop of malice.

"You said 'after she came back to the office.' From lunch, did you mean?"

"No, from the field."

"Field?"

"Investigating a claim. That's part of our job here."

"Do you remember which claim?"

"She was out on three that day, I believe."

"All here in the city?"

"Two were."

"And the third?"

"I don't recall."

"Can you tell me who the insurers were?"

"Oh, I couldn't," Ms. Fisher said. "That's confidential information."

"Couldn't you make an exception in this case? Given the circumstances?"

"No, I'm sorry." She said it firmly, and punctuated the refusal by lowering her voice and adding, "I could lose my job."

"I understand."

"I mean, I like Ms. Haas, I really do"—lying through her teeth; she didn't like Ms. Haas any more than I liked *her*—"but even to help her get an inheritance . . . no, I just couldn't take the chance."

I nodded and smiled and said, "Tell me this. Do you think

she's been seeing this new man regularly the past three weeks?"

"Oh, I'm sure she has. She still has that look. And she's been . . . well, more cheerful than usual."

"Right up to last Thursday?"

"Yes. You know, that *could* be why she decided to take her vacation so suddenly. Her and her . . . friend wanting to be alone somewhere together."

"Maybe so."

"I hope he's not married," Ms. Fisher lied.

"So do I." I got to my feet. "I won't take up any more of your time. Thanks for being so candid with me."

"Oh, I'm glad to help." She stood, too, smoothed her skirt over her bony hips. "I'd better show you the way out. It's something of a maze in here."

She showed me the way out. At the door to the reception area she said with a bright smile, "I hope you find her all right. And that she gets everything that's coming to her."

She wasn't fooling either of us. What she meant was, she hoped Grady Haas wasn't entitled to a penny. And that when I found her, it was in a highly compromising situation with a highly married man who had no intention of divorcing his wife.

Chapter **6**

TWENTY MINUTES after I left Intercoastal I was sitting in the Embarcadero Center offices of another insurance company, Great Western. Specifically, in the twenty-ninth floor sanctum of Great Western's chief claims adjuster, Barney Rivera.

Barney and I were old friends and poker adversaries. He had saved my tail more than once in lean times by throwing bits of business my way; I still got jobs from him more or less regularly, since Great Western was another of the small companies that did not employ a full-time investigative staff. Barney was a little guy, just a couple of inches over five feet. His polished rosewood desk was bigger than he was, so that sitting behind it he looked like somebody's nattily attired, mop-headed kid playing executive. He was also overweight, one of the reasons being an addiction to peppermint candy, and he owned a round, dimpled baby face and the most soulful pair of fawn eyes this side of the Disney version of *Bambi.* The overall effect was of a cute stuffed animal—a "cuddle bunny," as one of his lady friends had once dubbed him. Women just loved old Barney to pieces. Some wanted to mother him; others just wanted him. He hadn't lacked for feminine companionship for more than twenty-four hours during all the time I'd known him. Not surprisingly, Barney being Barney, he attributed his appeal to the fact that he was "hung like a horse." For all I knew, he was—but I hoped he wasn't. Life is unfair enough as it is.

"Your timing is lousy," he said. "I was just getting ready to go out for lunch." He scooped up a handful of peppermints from the dish on his desk. "I'll give you five minutes."

"I need a favor, Barney."

"Uh-huh. Why else would you show up like this?"

"Just a small one. It'll take you ten minutes . . . maybe fifteen."

He crunched a peppermint. "I'm listening."

"Some background first, so you'll know why I'm asking." I told him briefly about Grady Haas, what I'd found out from Lisa Fisher.

"No wonder you live hand-to-mouth," he said, "taking on that kind of job." But he wasn't being serious. He had a barbed wit and an equally barbed tongue; among those in our poker group he was known as Barney the Needle. "So where do I come in?"

"I figure maybe this guy Grady met three weeks ago has something to do with the trouble she's in. I can't find out who he is until I know which claims she was investigating on April Fools' Day. That's where you come in."

He looked at me. Ate another peppermint and looked at me some more.

"Oh come on, Barney," I said. "All you insurance people eat lunch together, hang out together. You think I don't know that? I wouldn't be surprised if you were sleeping with Intercoastal's CEO."

"Intercoastal's CEO is male."

"His secretary, then. Or, hell, his wife *and* his daughter, if he's got either one."

"He has. The wife's a dog but the daughter's not bad."

"So will you find out for me? Names, addresses, types of claims—that's all I need. A couple of telephone calls . . ."

"Says you. It's not that simple."

"But you *can* do it?"

Another peppermint disappeared inside Barney's chubby maw. "Yeah, I can do it. But not until after lunch. I'm already late," he said, looking at his watch, "and your five minutes are up."

"Who is she?" I asked him.

"Who?"

"The woman you're having lunch with?"

"Her name's Claudia. Hooters out to here." He grinned and made a shooing motion. "Don't call me, I'll call you."

"Thanks, Barney. Listen, before I go . . . I heard a good joke last night."

"Yeah? I hope it's short."

"It is."

I told him the jungle missionary position story. I expected a belly laugh; what I got was a scornful chuckle. And another jab from his needle.

"Kerry told you that one, right?"

"How'd you know that?"

"It's a woman's joke."

"A what?"

"Don't you see it? Wise career woman vanquishes dumb macho swordsman. Fem-lib stuff, script by Gloria Steinem."

"Oh, for Christ's sake, Barney. It's just a joke—a *funny* joke, I thought."

"Sure you did. She's got you brainwashed, pal."

"You know what you are, don't you?"

"Sure—a sexist pig. And proud of it."

"Barney, sometimes I wonder why I put up with you."

"You need me to do favors for you, that's why."

"No, cuddle bunny, it's because you're so damned *cute.*"

"Jealous, aren't we?" he said. Smugly, the bastard.

I went out. Dumb macho swordsman vanquishes wise male fem-libber.

I DROVE BACK to O'Farrell, put the car away in the parking garage down the block, and walked up to Zim's on Van Ness for a chef's salad. It was one-fifteen when I reopened for business. The office was shut up tight; Christ knew where Eberhardt was, or what kind of crazy new nuptial scheme he was hatching; he hadn't bothered to leave word. Three messages on my machine, two pertaining to cases I was working on and the other from Kerry.

She was just back from lunch, and in good spirits, when I returned her call. Things were continuing to look up on the Cybil front. The Marin seniors' complex had impressed her mother last night, and while she wasn't ready yet to make a commitment, Kerry thought she was leaning in that direction. An equally optimistic report had come this morning from the member of Children of Grieving Parents who'd acted as Cybil's escort.

"I've got a feeling," Kerry said, "my apartment will be mine again before summer."

"But not your bed."

"Uh-huh. Making plans already."

"Well, you know us Italians."

"Don't I, though. It's a good thing Cybil doesn't know about that part of our relationship or she'd never leave. She warned me about men like you once, when I was about fourteen."

"Didn't listen though, did you?"

"And aren't you glad I didn't?"

I spent most of the afternoon on the telephone, finishing up part of my caseload. And doing a preemployment screening job of Eberhardt's, because he was still among the missing and because the client called and wanted to know what was taking so long. Most of the work we do is skip-tracing, insurance investigation, or preemployment screening, and that means a lot of telephone time. Contrary to popular opinion, modern private detectives worry more about secretary's spread than they do about getting shot, beaten up, or whacked on the cranium.

I also took two calls for Eberhardt concerning the wedding. The first was from the guy in charge of the hall on Church Street where the reception was to be held; he said they were having trouble finding a dais and would it be okay if the band just set up on the floor itself. What band? I said. The band Mr. Eberhardt hired, he said—The Grenadiers. Oh, I said. Band, I thought; what next? The second call was from the caterer, who proceeded to tell me what next. He'd been assured that the wedding cake would be ready in time, he said, even though it *had* been ordered virtually at the last minute and *did* require considerable preparation. Why did it require considerable preparation? I asked. Well, he said, Mario's Wedding Confection Supreme *was* three-tiered, after all, and the deluxe latticework arbor intertwined with sugar roses that would surmount it *did* have to be special-ordered. Oh yes, he said, and would I please tell Mr. Eberhardt that Mario also assured him the absolute largest bride and groom figures that would fit inside the arbor were six inches in height.

I was still thinking about Mario's Wedding Confection Supreme and the deluxe latticework arbor intertwined with sugar roses when Barney finally called at twenty of four. "I hope you've got something to tell me that I want to hear," I said. "I've had enough negative input this afternoon."

"Having a bad day, are we?"

"I've had better. You going to make it worse?"

"Nope. Grady Haas was working on three claims as of April Fools' Day. One was over in Port Costa, but she didn't go out there until the following day. The two she investigated on the first are local. One—Savarese Importing, Vernon Savarese, owner, 4879 China Basin Street; damaged shipment of goods from Taiwan. Two—Holloway and Company, Marine

Electronics, Lloyd Holloway, prop., Pier Twenty-eight; water damage from burst pipes. You get all that?"

"Got it," I said.

"Here's something else, a little bonus," Barney said. "Lady I talked to at Intercoastal happens to work in personnel. Seems a man called her up yesterday, asking for information about Grady Haas. Where she could be reached, names and addresses of any close relatives. Said he was her fiancé and had urgent business with her. He didn't get anywhere, naturally."

"He give a name?"

"David Jones. Phony, probably."

"Yeah," I said.

I told him I'd see him on Saturday—he'd been one of the first to be invited to the wedding (which I now thought of as Eberhardt's Folly)—and rang off.

David Jones. The same person who'd searched Grady's apartment? Odds on. And maybe what he'd been after there was the same thing he'd been after from Intercoastal's personnel department. Maybe it wasn't anything Grady had that he wanted; maybe it was Grady herself.

THE PORT OF SAN FRANCISCO has been in existence for nearly a hundred and thirty years, ever since the days of Pacific Mail Steamship Lines' "China Clipper" trade. Time was, it was *the* major port on the Pacific Rim: hundreds of thousands of steamship passengers and billions of dollars' worth of cargo poured in and out annually; throngs of longshoremen—one of them my old man, in the thirties—worked day and night along its seven-and-a-half miles of waterfront. No more. The Port of Oakland gradually began enticing shippers across the bay, and in the seventies became an aggressive leader in containerization. Other West Coast ports—Tacoma, Long Beach, L.A.—flourished in the container shipping market as well. Not the Port of San Francisco. Thanks to a poor location for containerization purposes, plus labor disputes, feuding commissioners, lack of foresight, and general apathy, it developed into the coast's one big maritime loser. And as a result helped bring about the demise of its biggest customer, the once mighty Pacific Far East Lines.

It's doubtful that the port will ever again regain prominence, although there is a plan in the works to deepen a pair of hundred-year-old Southern Pacific tunnels near Hunters Point and use them to transport double-stacked container cars by rail from the Embarcadero up through the Sierras and into middle America. More likely, the waterfront will one day lose its blue-collar identity altogether, become a bland upscale mecca for tourists and yuppies. Pier 39, a tourist complex of restaurants and shops built several years ago, has been hugely profitable and has paved the way for other projects by wealthy developers: hotels, conference centers, luxury condos. Some of these have already been built; others, such as a fancy hotel and marina at Piers 24 and 26, have received approval from the port commissioners. Big money talks—loud and fast. And the port needs money now more than ever, to cover an estimated fifty million dollars in repairs to piers and buildings damaged by the recent 7.1 earthquake. Environmentalists don't like what's happening to the waterfront; the fishermen and various historical preservation and public interest groups don't like it; most of the city's residents, me included, don't like it. But unless the expensive tunnel plan somehow comes to pass, nothing and nobody is going to stop it.

Pier 28, the closest of the two addresses Barney Rivera had given me, was just south of the closed-off section of the Embarcadero between Mission and Folsom, where the double-decked Embarcadero Freeway extension curves inland from the waterfront. The freeway structure also suffered damage in the October '89 quake, most severely in that two-block area; it, too, has been closed to traffic since, its unstable decks shored up with wooden platforms, while the city makes up its mind to rebuild or knock the whole thing down. Congestion had come to the area when Bayside Village, one of the new downtown condo complexes, went up across from Pier 28 a while back; now, with the blocked street and detours, traffic was perpetually snarled and parking was at a premium. I had to leave my car well up on Bryant, in the shadow of the Bay Bridge approach, and hoof it three blocks to the pier.

Holloway & Company, Marine Electronics, was a small, weathered building tucked in between the main pier warehouse and the funky Boondocks Restaurant. A sign on its front said they specialized in ship-to-shore radio telephones, depth sounders, fish finders, speed and wind instruments, and Loran navigational equipment. Inside, I found Lloyd Holloway in a cluttered alcove that served as his office. He was a cheerful, balding man about my age, friendly and cooperative.

"Sure, I remember the woman from Intercoastal," he said. "Haas, is it? She wasn't here more than half an hour. Approved our claim right off, didn't have any reason not to. One look at those pipes in our warehouse and the ruined stock, anybody could see we were entitled to damages."

"Did you deal with her yourself, Mr. Holloway?"

"I did. Nice polite young woman."

"She talk to anyone else while she was here?"

"No, just me. How come you're asking? She in some kind of trouble or something?"

"Just a routine investigation. One more question and I'll be on my way. What time of day was she here, do you recall?"

"Sure. Right after lunch. One o'clock."

One down, one to go . . .

China Basin Street is on the waterfront a mile or so south of Pier 28, between Third Street and the bay. This section used to be one of the hubs of the city's marine commerce; now it gave bitter and graphic testimony to the port's deterioration. There were still a few small shipping companies in operation here, and a handful of marine outfitters and engineering firms; and over at the big dry docks and repair yards at Mission Rock Terminal, half a dozen freighters were being attended to. But the atmosphere was nonetheless one of abandonment and decay. Portions of the old, rotting China Basin piers had been buckled and cracked open by the quake, but even before that they had sat unused except as perches for flocking gulls; now they were separated from the street by fences plastered with DANGER—KEEP OUT signs. On the inland side, the network of Southern Pacific spur tracks that had once serviced the piers were rusting and weed-choked. Hulks and pieces of boats were strewn about, in and out of the water, shorn of everything of value by the owners of the salvage yards that proliferated along this end of the waterfront. Parked along the street were scabrous cars and vans crammed full of personal belongings— the temporary domains of some of the city's homeless.

Savarese Importing was a perfect match for its surroundings. It sat by itself between a salvage yard and one of the venerable private boat clubs that have inhabited the basin for decades—an old two-story warehouse with a slanted sheetmetal roof, sheetmetal siding, and a wood-and-tarpaper facade reduced by fog and wind to a warped, pocked gray. A black iron fence enclosed a parking area in front; behind the building was a stubby pier that seemed to have survived the October temblor more or less intact.

It was colder here than it had been at Pier 28, with nothing on either side of the warehouse to deflect the wind that came knifing in across the bay. The odor of brine and fish was sharper here too. I didn't waste any time going through the unlocked gate and across the parking area and into the warehouse.

Gloomy place, illuminated by wire-shaded bulbs hanging at the ends of long drop cords. Along the entire north wall and part of the rear wall was an ell-shaped second floor that took up about half of the interior; the other half was open all the way up to the girdered roof. The front third of the ell wall had windows cut in it so that people upstairs could look down at what was going on below. A rickety-looking staircase led up there. Straight ahead I could see a shipping counter, the rear loading doors, stacks and pallets of wooden crates and cardboard drums with Chinese characters stencilled on them. The brine smell was in here, too, mixed with odors of creosote and mold. So was the cold. The warehouse temperature wasn't more than a few degrees above the temperature outside.

A couple of men were working at the rear, one of them piloting a midget forklift; a third man, bundled in coat and sweater and cap, stood leaning on a hand truck nearby. Killing the last few minutes until quitting time, I thought. It was almost five o'clock.

I went over to the idle one. He didn't strike me as a likely candidate for Grady Haas's mystery man—middle-aged, not particularly good-looking, not particularly bright if his expression was an accurate barometer—but I asked him about her anyway.

"The insurance broad, yeah," he said. "Nice hair, okay face, but not much in the tit department. Cool, too—one of them iceberg types, you know what I mean?"

"Did you talk to her?"

"Nah. Why should I?"

"Who did talk to her?"

He shrugged. "Just the boss, far as I know."

I asked him if Vernon Savarese was around and he said upstairs in the office, just go on up. I started away, paused, came back, gestured at the cluttered floor space, and asked if he minded telling me what it was they imported from Taiwan. He didn't seem surprised at the question. Curiosity ran shallow in him—almost as shallow as his stream of consciousness.

"Party crap," he said.

"How's that again?"

"You know, kids and adults have a party, they want party crap. Paper hats, noisemakers, confetti, birthday candles— crap like that. Used to be people wanted it, anyhow. Not so much these days."

"Business slow, is it?"

"You said it, man. We got crap here we can't give away. Sign of the times, you know what I mean?"

"Not exactly."

"The freakin' government," he said. "Who wants to buy party crap, have parties, when he's got the freakin' government on his ass about taxes all the time?"

I left him contemplating his sociopolitical theories and went up the narrow staircase to the second-floor ell. The office was at the front, a one-room, windowless enclosure behind a fire door; the rest of the ell seemed to be more cluttered storage space. There were two people in the office, a thin birdlike woman and a fat, dark-haired guy in his forties wearing red suspenders over a green-striped shirt. The fat man turned out to be Vernon Savarese. He let me have a glad-hander's smile until I presented him with one of my business cards; then he scowled so hard his thick eyebrows seemed to fold down into the bridge of his nose.

"A detective?" he said. "What's a detective want with me?"

I told him what it was I wanted. His scowl faded and his jowly face reshaped itself into relieved lines; he made a rumbling sound that I supposed was a laugh.

"Jeez," he said, "you had me going there for a minute. I thought maybe my ex-wife was trying to hassle me again. Blood out of a turnip, for Chrissake. Take your last goddamn dime if you let 'em."

"Nothing like that, Mr. Savarese. You do remember Grady Haas?"

"Sure, sure. The damaged-shipment claim."

"You dealt with her yourself, is that right?"

"Who else? It's my company, my name's on the policy."

"How long was she here?"

"Hour, maybe a little more."

"Did she talk to anyone else besides you?"

"Anyone else?"

"One of your employees. Or somebody who happened to be here at the time."

"Well . . . Mabel over there. My bookkeeper."

"Just you and Mabel?"

"That's it. How come you want to know that?"

"It pertains to my investigation. Just routine."

"Yeah? Doesn't have to do with the claim, does it?"

"No, it doesn't."

"What I mean, she approved it," Savarese said. "Not the full amount, but hell, I expected that. That's not gonna change, is it? I'm still gonna get the money?"

"I can't answer that, Mr. Savarese. I don't work for Intercoastal Insurance."

"Yeah, right, so you said. Not for Intercoastal and not for my ex-wife. Who do you work for?"

"I can't answer that either. Thanks for your time."

"Sure, no problem. You find out what you wanted to know?"

"No," I said, "not yet."

Two down, none to go. Grady Haas evidently hadn't met her mystery man at either of the claim sites she'd visited on April Fools' Day. Which meant that she might have crossed his path at lunch somewhere, or bumped into him on the street, or met him in dozens of other ways and places. So? So.

How do you go about tracing the movements of a close-mouthed loner on a day three weeks gone?

Chapter 7

I DROVE BACK to Twenty-first Street, to see if I could pry Todd Bellin out of his flat and some information out of him. But leaning on his doorbell got me exactly what it had earlier: nothing. The only difference was that this time the muslin drapes stayed tightly drawn when I walked away and for the ten minutes I sat watching them from inside my car.

Getting on toward six o'clock by then. I took the car up to Mission and out toward Geneva, to a Mexican restaurant I know that serves a fine *carne asada,* made with a cream and sweet-onion sauce. It's a high-calorie, high-cholesterol dish, but I was in a mood to indulge myself tonight. Besides, I'd kept my weight down for over a year now, ate sensibly ninety-five percent of the time and maintained a regular exercise program. A little treat now and then is what makes life worth living. It also provides a measure of guilt, which makes you work twice as hard afterward to offset any damaging effects it might have . . . and if that wasn't a pretty fair rationalization for an occasional face-stuffing, it would do until a better one came along.

The carne asada was as good as ever; so were the salad and chile relleno and refried beans that went with it. At seven-fifteen, feeling fat and guilty, I drove back to Twenty-first Street for one more pass at Todd Bellin.

There was light showing now behind the drawn drapes of his flat. Or there was until I pulled up down the block and cut the engine; then the window over there went dark.

Hunched up against the night wind, I hurried across the street. But not to his building—to the one next to it. A tunnel-like driveway passed under that one, into a courtyard parking area. One pace inside the tunnel, up against the wall, and I was in thick shadow; but I could still see the front of Bellin's building. He might have switched off his front-room lights because he was moving into another part of the flat. Then again he might be going out somewhere, in which case I was now in a good position to brace him when he showed.

Three or four minutes passed. The tunnel was not much shelter against the wind that came whipping through from street to courtyard, making my ears burn. It also carried the aroma of somebody's Mexican cooking, which made my stomach ache and produced a couple of unsatisfactory belches. I thought: Hell, he's not going to come out. He's forted up in there for the night.

So then, in the perverse way of things, I heard his door open. And a couple of seconds later I saw the dark shape of a man lean out from the vestibule.

He looked upstreet first, which gave me time to ease a half-step deeper into the shadows. It was another few seconds before he ventured onto the sidewalk, moving in the opposite direction from where I was in a stride that was oddly stiff and jerky, as if he was injured in some way and hurting. I came out of the tunnel after him, walking soft. He didn't go far, just to where a car—a light-colored compact of some kind—was parked under a flickery streetlamp fifty feet away. The driver's door was locked; he bent to it, awkwardly, to use his key. I quit trying to be stealthy and quickened my pace.

When he heard me coming I was only a few paces from him. He wheeled around, in movements that were almost spastic, and the look on his face surprised me: it was one of stark terror. I heard his keys jangle as they hit the sidewalk. If he hadn't lost his grip on them he might have tried to run; as it was he stood frozen on the edge of flight, one hand up in front of him as if warding off a blow.

By then I was close enough for a second surprise: The left side of his face was bruised, lacerated; a two-inch scabbed cut ran up his cheek from the corner of his mouth, pulling his lips out of shape. Around his neck was the kind of brace you wear when you've suffered whiplash or cartilage damage.

"Mr. Bellin? Todd Bellin?"

He shook his head, but it wasn't the name he was denying. "Who are you?" he said in a thin, cracking voice. "What do you want?"

"To talk to you, ask you a few questions."

"About what?"

"Your relationship with Grady Haas—"

He reacted as violently as if I'd thrown a punch at him. He stumbled back against the car, braced himself against it with both arms thrust up and out like a man about to be crucified. "Oh God," he said, "leave me alone, don't hurt me again."

"I'm not going to hurt you. Take it easy."

He didn't seem to hear that; he was listening to the voice of his own terror. "I don't know where she is, I swear to God I don't know!"

I wanted to shake him, but that was not the way to get him calmed down; if I put my hands on him he was liable to start screaming. Instead I backed off a step, said his name twice, softly. Then I said, "Listen to me. I'm not going to hurt you. I'm not the person who hurt you before. You understand?"

He heard that, I thought, but he didn't believe it yet.

"I'm a detective," I said. "Working to help Grady." I got my wallet out, doing it slow so as not to panic him, flipped it open to the Photostat of my license and held it up in front of his face. There wasn't enough light for him to see the license clearly, but I thought the gesture itself might be enough. "See? A detective, Mr. Bellin. Trying to help Grady. I don't mean you any harm."

He stared at the Photostat, or in the direction of the Photostat—not moving his head or his eyes. Then, all at once, his muscles relaxed and he sagged so heavily against the car that he had to grab hold of the door handle to keep from falling down. I could hear his breath rattling in his throat.

I bent, picked up his keys, held them out to him. His fingers, when he finally took the keyring, were as wet as if he'd dunked them in water. I said, "Let's go inside and talk. Unless there's someplace important you have to go. . . ."

"No," he said, "no, I . . . some food, there's nothing left to eat."

"You can go shopping later, all right? After we talk."

". . . All right."

He pushed away from the car. He was wobbly on his pins but I still didn't touch him; I backed off and walked alongside him, not too close, to the vestibule of his building. I hung back there, too, on the sidewalk, so as not to crowd him in the tight dark space. He had some trouble getting his key into the door lock. When I heard the latch click I moved ahead, just in case he had some idea of trying to rush inside and slam the door between us. But there was neither aggression nor defiance in him. He flipped on a light, revealing a narrow stairwell and a set of carpeted stairs, and without touching the door or looking back at me he started up—both feet on each step, leaning on the handrail like an old man.

I shut the door, went up after him. At the top was a short hallway; he put on more lights, turned left and entered the front room with the drawn muslin drapes. Living room, not too big, dominated by electronic equipment: stereo, CD player, tape deck, speakers, TV and VCR. He sank onto a lumpy plaid couch and folded his hands together and held them tight between his knees. On an end table near him was an

8 by 10 color photograph of two people smiling at each other in a moderate closeup; he was one, Grady Haas was the other. Displayed as it was, the photo told me that his feelings for her still ran deep.

I sat on the edge of a chair across from him. His head was bowed; he didn't seem to want to look at me. He was about thirty, blond, pale, slightly built inside the bulky pea jacket and chinos he wore. Not particularly attractive, but there was a boyish, ascetic quality to the arrangement of his features that a certain kind of woman—Grady Haas's kind—would find appealing.

Somebody had done a job on him, all right, somebody who knew how to inflict pain without breaking bones. Working on just the one side of his face and the neck area, concentrating the hurt. Three, maybe four days ago, I thought. The discoloration from the bruises was starting to fade a little, there was no longer any swelling around the blackened eye, and the cut at the corner of the mouth was scabbed and healing.

The silence had thickened enough to make him lift his head stiffly and flick a glance my way. Then he fixed his gaze on his lap, on his pale hands moving against each other between his knees. The hands were unmarked; he hadn't done any damage to his assailant. Or even tried to, I thought. Not a fighter, Todd Bellin, in any sense of the term. Passive type; possibly a coward. Victim with a capital *V.*

I said, "Tell me what happened, Mr. Bellin."

Nothing for a little while. Then, "Saturday night . . . I went to a movie. He was here when I got back . . . waiting for me."

"Inside, you mean?"

"Yes. Waiting in the dark."

"How'd he get in?"

"A window in back . . . there's a service porch. . . ." Bellin drew a deep, shuddery breath. "He'd unscrewed the light bulb over the stairs. I thought it was burned out and I came up and he . . . he was waiting. He grabbed me around the neck. He had a gun . . . he said if I didn't tell him what he wanted to know he'd kill me."

"What did he want to know?"

"Where he could find Grady. If her folks were alive, if she has any sisters or brothers or other relatives. I told him I didn't know, I hadn't seen or talked to her in months, and she never talked about herself anyway, she was always so secretive . . . but he wouldn't listen, he just started beating me. Asking the same questions over and over and hurting me, he wouldn't stop hurting me. . . ."

"You have any idea who he is?"

"No. No."

"What did he look like?"

"I don't know. The whole time . . . in the dark . . ."

"His size, then. Big, small, fat, lean, tall, short?"

"Big," Bellin said, "he was big. Not fat, just . . . big. Strong. He dragged me down the hall, he almost broke my neck. . . ."

"What about his voice?"

". . . I don't know what you mean."

"Was there anything distinctive about it? Did he have an accent? Speak nasally? Anything like that?"

"No. It was just a voice . . . God, I don't remember, I don't want to remember." He shuddered, remembering. Sweat had run down into his eyes; he knuckled it away.

"Why did he think you'd know where Grady is?"

"He knew we'd dated, that I asked her to marry me last year. I don't know how but he knew."

Something he found in her apartment, maybe, I thought. "Did he give you any idea of why he wants to find her?"

"No."

"Something he let slip, a hint?"

"No."

"All right," I said. "He kept on asking you questions, kept on hitting you. Then what?"

"I . . . passed out. I couldn't take it anymore."

"Was he still here when you came to?"

"No, he was gone."

"What condition was the place in?"

"My things . . . thrown around. He'd been through everything while I was unconscious."

More likely he'd done the searching before Bellin got home. If he'd found what he was after, he wouldn't have waited around; he'd have been long gone. But I asked the question anyway: "Did you have anything of Grady's that might lead him to her?"

He shook his head. "She didn't leave me with anything. Except this," and he reached out to touch the framed photograph.

"You call the police, file a report with them?"

"I didn't dare. I didn't even go across the street to the hospital to see about my neck. I've had this brace for years . . . a car accident once . . ."

"He told you not to notify the police?"

"While he was hitting me. He said if I did, if I told anybody he'd been asking about Grady, he'd come back and . . . he'd . . ." Bellin shuddered again. The fear had made his voice as brittle as old glass; and when he flicked another glance my way I could see it hot and curdled in his eyes. "What if he . . . what if he finds out I told you?"

"He won't," I said flatly.

"You don't know how terrified I've been that he'd come back. I've hardly slept since it happened. When you were here earlier and rang the bell . . . I thought you might be . . ."

"Yeah. But you're still here anyway. Why didn't you go stay with relatives or a friend?"

"Looking the way I do? I'd have to explain . . . I couldn't do that. And what if he does come back? It might be worse if he couldn't find me . . . he might do what he threatened to . . . oh God!"

"So you've been holed up here since Saturday night, licking your wounds."

"What else could I do?" He was close to tears now.

You could be a man, I thought. But I didn't say it. I got to my feet, and the movement made him lift his head again.

"You're really a detective?" he said.

"That's what I am."

"Trying to help Grady, you said. Because of . . . *him*?"

"Yes."

"He hasn't found her . . . hurt her . . . ?"

"Not so far," I said.

"Then you know where she is? Is she safe?"

"She's not your concern, Bellin."

"She should be, we should have been married. . . ." There was a tear on his cheek now; it made one of the healing bruises look glazed and shiny. "I've been worried sick about her," he said. "I called her apartment that night, as hurt as I was. And her office yesterday, but all they'd tell me is that she's on vacation."

I didn't say anything.

"I love her," he said. "I still love her. I can't stand the idea of anything happening to her."

Sure, I thought. So you didn't call the police; so you've been cowering in here the past three days. And when he was hitting you, hurting you, you'd have told him where Grady was if you'd known. Damn right you would have. In ten seconds flat.

"I don't understand any of this," Bellin said miserably. "A man like that, an animal . . . why would somebody like him be after Grady?"

"That's what I'm trying to find out."

For the first time he made eye contact. "Don't let him hurt her. Please don't let him hurt her."

There was nothing for me to say to that. I turned away from him, toward the hallway.

"Tell her I love her," he said. "Will you do that? Tell her I'll always love her, no matter what. . . ."

I went out of there thinking: Things could be even worse for her than they are. She could have said yes to Bellin's proposal.

Chapter **8**

ALL THE WAY HOME I brooded. It was one thing to speculate that Grady Haas might be in danger, another to find her apartment searched, still another to see and hear what had been done to Todd Bellin. Somebody was after her, all right, there was no doubt of that now—somebody to whom violence came easy, who was brutal, methodical, relentless. A psychopath, possibly; a hardcase almost certainly. The mystery man she'd met on April Fools' Day? Someone connected with the mystery man? Someone else entirely?

One thing I could be sure of: He hadn't quit looking for her, whoever he was, and he wouldn't until he found her or I found him. Men like that are even more focused, and much more implacable, than men like me; they don't frustrate. Grady may have lived in a narrow little world the past dozen years, but even though she didn't talk to anyone about her roots, not even a man who'd proposed marriage to her, neither had she made any effort to hide her background. Sooner or later he'd get a whiff of the farm in San Bernado. You did not have to be a trained skip-tracer to track somebody down; all you needed was cunning, dedication, the person's name, and some knowledge of who he or she is.

That was what put him one big step ahead of me. I had no idea who *he* was, not even a description to go on. Nor any idea of the why of it—what had happened last Thursday night or early Friday to send Grady running home to San Bernado and him into an urgent hunt for her. Only Grady herself knew the answers, and maybe even she didn't realize how deadly the situation was. I had to have her cooperation to even out the odds; without it, trying to work blind, there was damned little I could do to help her.

As soon as I came into the flat, I went to the telephone. Arlo Haas answered almost immediately, as if he'd been sitting with his hand on the receiver.

"Can you talk?" I asked him.

"Grady's upstairs in her room."

"Everything all right, then?"

"Same as before."

"No telephone calls for her, no visitors?"

"No." He'd picked up on the tension in my voice; I could hear tension in his, too, now. "What is it? What'd you find out?"

I told him, holding nothing back, not trying to sugarcoat any of it. He didn't speak when I was done. The line was dead quiet; I could not even hear him breathing.

"Mr. Haas?"

"I'm here," he said in a thin voice. "I better go talk to her right now."

"Tell her what happened to Todd Bellin. About hiring me, too, if you have to. Whatever it takes to get the truth out of her."

"Where're you? Home?"

"Yes. The number's on my business card. One other thing, Mr. Haas."

"Go ahead."

"I don't think Grady ought to keep on staying there with

you. He hasn't found out about the farm yet; that doesn't mean he won't."

"I got a twelve-gauge shotgun," Haas said grimly. "He comes around here, I'll blow his fucking head off."

"I believe it. But you can't spend every minute with her, and you can't keep an eye on every door and window."

"Damn cripple," he said, but there was no bitterness or self-pity in the words; only anger.

"I didn't mean that. I meant you're only one man . . . just the two of you there alone."

"Gus too. He's a good watchdog."

"Still. There must be someplace else she can stay."

"Well, Mary Ellen Crowley."

"No. She'd be too easy to find out about."

"My housekeeper, then. Mexican woman, Constanza Vargas, lives with her husband in San Lucas. She'll do it if I ask her."

"Good. Tonight, if you can arrange it. Otherwise, as soon as possible."

"If you think it's best."

I went into the kitchen, feeling fidgety, and opened a beer and paced around with it. Ten minutes passed; fifteen. It was after nine now. I wanted another beer, talked myself out of it. To have something to do I opened up the record cabinet and poked through my jazz albums—an activity I hadn't indulged in for a while. I used to listen to jazz regularly, but as sometimes happens with minor hobbies I had drifted away from music in recent years. Kerry playing the Miles Davis album last night had reminded me of what I'd been missing.

Dixieland had always been my favorite; gutbucket, the hotter the better. I found an old Jelly Roll Morton reissue and put it on the stereo. I was listening to "Cannon Ball Blues," Jelly Roll's piano solo with the horns ad-libbing, the sweet steady beat taking some of the edge out of me, when the telephone rang.

That brought the edge right back. I shut the volume down

before I answered, but it wasn't Arlo Haas's voice I heard; it was Kerry's.

"The wedding's off," she said.

"What?"

"Bobbie Jean just called me. She and Eb had a big fight tonight—I mean a *big* fight. She gave him back his ring."

"Oh boy. What started the fight?"

"He finally went too far. Did you know he'd ordered a huge wedding cake?"

"Not until this afternoon."

"And hired a band to play at the reception?"

"The Grenadiers. Yeah."

"And somebody to videotape the whole thing?"

". . . No."

"And a chauffeured limo to take them from the church to the reception and from the reception to the airport?"

"My God."

"Bobbie Jean didn't know about any of this until tonight," Kerry said. "She hit the roof when he told her. All that extravagance—and he doesn't have nearly enough saved to pay for it all. She doesn't want to go into a third marriage several thousand dollars in debt. I don't blame her."

"Neither do I."

"She told him the only way she'll marry him now is in a civil ceremony, the way she wanted to do it in the beginning. He wouldn't hear of it; you know how he is. They ended up screaming at each other and she returned the ring and walked out."

"She's upset tonight, sure, but maybe tomorrow . . ."

"No, her mind's made up. She said she won't back down and I think she means it. She's already started calling people to tell them the wedding's off."

"Terrific," I said. "When Eb hears about that it'll ensure *he* doesn't back down. His pride won't let him."

"He'll listen to you sometimes," Kerry said.

"Not about something like this."

"You'd better talk to him anyway."

"Yeah. Listen, babe, I'm expecting a business call. After it comes I'll call Eb and then get back to you. Half hour or so, all right?"

She said all right and we rang off. I started out of the bedroom, grumbling to myself, taking Eberhardt's name in vain; the phone rang again before I was through the doorway. This time the voice on the other end belonged to Arlo Haas. And the news he had for me wasn't good.

"She won't talk about it," he said. He was on the raw edge; I could hear it in his voice. "Won't tell me who he is or why he's after her."

"Why not?"

"Just keeps saying it don't matter, she don't care anymore if he finds her."

"You make sense out of that?"

"None, dammit, and I'm her father."

"You tell her what happened to Bellin?"

"I told her. Said she was sorry, that's all."

"How'd she react when you told her about me?"

"Didn't react. Just looked at me and said, 'You shouldn't have done that, Daddy,' but not as if she cared."

"She say anything at all about the man?"

"Not a word," Haas said. "I tried everything—pleading with her to shaking her till her teeth rattled. None of it done a lick of good."

"What about getting her away from there? Will she go?"

"She don't want to."

"Can you get her out anyway?"

"If I have to drag her," he said. "Nobody home at the Vargas place when I called, but I'll fix it up with Constanza when she gets home. Grady'll be in San Lucas by noon tomorrow, one way or another."

"Good. That buys us a little more time." I paused. "You might want to think about getting away for a while yourself, Mr. Haas."

"No, I'm staying put. He shows up, I want to be here to greet him. Me and Gus and my twelve-gauge."

I didn't argue with him. It was his home, his decision. He said, "What're the chances of you finding him first?"

"Straight answer? Not good. I haven't got anything to go on—no description, no leads."

Haas was silent.

I said, "Keep working on Grady. Try to get something out of her that I can work with."

"I will."

"Call me if you do get something. Anytime tonight. Otherwise I'll check in with you in the morning."

The fidgets were back; I did some more pacing to work them off. This new wrinkle was puzzling as well as frustrating. Why wouldn't Grady care that a man was hunting her, evidently with the intention of doing her harm? It had to be an intensely personal reason, one that was tangled up in whatever her relationship was with the man; nothing else made sense. So she had to know him . . . intimately, as a lover? The mystery man? In any case he had to have done something pretty terrible to shatter her long-standing defenses. Without the what and why, I couldn't find who; without who, I couldn't find what and why. . . .

On one of my passes through the kitchen I noticed the clock on the stove. Quarter of ten. Eberhardt, I thought. I went into the bedroom and called his home number, listened to the line make empty sounds for half a minute. Either he wasn't answering his phone or he was out somewhere soaking his injured pride in an alcohol bath. Eb doesn't drink much, and when he does set out to tie one on he doesn't drink well. He gets maudlin and sloppy and has a tendency to show up on friends' doorsteps in the middle of the night, looking for a shoulder to cry on. That would be all I'd need tonight.

I rang up Kerry. She said hopefully, "Maybe he went over to Bobbie Jean's to try to patch things up."

"Fat chance. The hat-in-hand apology isn't his style."

"Well, I'll call her anyhow. I might as well work on her until you have a chance to work on him." She sighed. "Isn't this fun?"

"Like a compound fracture."

"Marriage," she said. "Sucks," she said.

She was gone before I could think of a suitable rebuttal. At the moment I was no longer sure there was one.

I listened to some more of the Jelly Roll Morton album, without any pleasure. Arlo Haas didn't call back. Neither did Kerry. At ten-thirty I tried Eberhardt's number again; still no answer.

At eleven I went to bed. But not to sleep. It wasn't Eberhardt and his botched wedding that kept me awake; he'd brought it all on himself and I couldn't work up much sympathy for him. It was Grady Haas and her botched life. Little Miss Lonesome—a woman who had never really lived and who was already half dead inside at the age of thirty-one. Who could sleep with somebody like that huddled in a corner of his mind?

Chapter 9

I STILL FELT FIDGETY in the morning. But it was an undercurrent of restlessness, like a low-grade virus. For months after my abduction I had suffered random attacks of claustrophobia —days when I would awaken tense, sweaty, with goblin shapes hovering in the corners of my mind. Days, or parts of days, when I could barely function; when I would need to go for long aimless drives or walks in open-air places until the trapped, desperate feeling finally wore off. It had been a while now since I'd had one of those crippling spells; most of the time I could almost believe that I was through with them for good. Then a morning like this one came along, a ghostly reminder of those bad dead days, and of the fact that I wasn't really healed and never would be.

I cut my daily exercise program in half, made quick work of shower, shave, and dressing, and drank my coffee while I used the phone. I tried Eberhardt's number first. This time I got his answering machine, which meant that he'd made it home all right last night and that he was probably nursing a hangover this morning. It was just as well; I was not in the mood yet to confront him or his pigheadedness.

Arlo Haas had nothing to tell me, except that he'd made arrangements with Constanza Vargas and Grady was already on her way to San Lucas. He'd hammered at Grady for two more hours last night, without getting through to her; she simply wouldn't talk about her trouble, just kept begging him to leave her alone. This morning she'd hardly spoken. Hadn't even argued about leaving the farm. When Mrs. Vargas came, Grady had gotten in the car and sat there straight and stiff as they drove off. Like somebody being taken away to prison, Haas said.

It was just eight-thirty when I left the flat. Too early to open up the office; there wasn't anything for me to do there anyway except routine work. So I drove out past the U.S.F. campus to Temescal Terrace. I hadn't spoken to Grady's neighbors yet and maybe one of them would still be home this early. They were the only avenue I had left to explore.

Just as yesterday, I had to park around the corner on Turk Street. And just as yesterday, I got no response when I rang the bells under the cards labeled Voorhees and M. Norman/ C. Tagliozzi. This day was starting the way the last one had ended.

Now what?

I sat in the car and thought about it. The more I thought, the more stymied I felt. And the more stymied I felt, the more restless I became. The whole day stretched out emptily ahead of me. What was I going to do to fill it?

Drive down to San Lucas, I thought. Talk to Grady, see if *you* can pry some answers out of her.

I tried to talk myself out of the idea. Another three hundred miles of driving, round trip, and it would likely turn out to be a waste of time. She wouldn't talk to her own father; how was a stranger going to get her to open up? No sense in going all that distance, at the expense of the work piled up in the office—Eberhardt's as well as mine, and never mind that it was just routine. Stay home, put the day to some productive use.

It was a good argument, sound, well-reasoned, but I didn't listen to it. I was going; I'd been going from the first. Obsessive-compulsive, that was me. I'd always had a tendency that way, and in the past year it had been heightened. Give me a certain kind of job, one with a client like Arlo Haas and pieces that did not slot easily into established patterns, and I was off like a hound after a fox—run, keep on running, and damn everything else until I caught what I was chasing. Not a healthy way to do business, but there it was. You are what you are; circumstances only sharpen the edges.

The old hound fired up his Detroit legs and went racing south out of the city.

HOTTER IN THE SALINAS VALLEY today than it had been on Monday. No more populated, though; the illusion of a sleepy, dusty chunk of Steinbeckian landscape half-forgotten by time remained unchanged. But I felt no kinship with the valley this morning, no pleasurable sense of nostalgia. It was just a long, long stretch of parched hills and green fields and black asphalt—miles of emptiness to get through on the way to someplace else.

I BYPASSED SAN LUCAS and went to see Arlo Haas first. I needed Constanza Vargas's address, for one thing; and for another I wanted to look through Grady's car, something I should have done on Monday even though Haas hadn't found anything when he'd searched it.

When I drove into the farmyard he was sitting on the porch, in the shade of the second-story gallery, with Gus the black Lab on one side of him and his twelve-gauge shotgun on the other. The strain was telling on him; I could see that as soon as I got up close. He seemed shrunken, older, his eyes pouched with weariness, the stroke-stiffened side of his face even more lopsided. Candidate for another stroke, maybe a fatal one this time. The thought made me sadder, angrier, even more determined.

If he was surprised to see me, he didn't show it or express it. When I told him why I was there he nodded and said, "Thought it might be a good idea myself, you talking to Grady, but I didn't want to be telling you your business. You know what you're doing."

Sure I do, I thought. About half the time, on good days. Just like everybody else.

He gave me the Vargases' address, told me how to get there. He'd call Constanza and tell her I was coming, he said, while I had my look at Grady's car.

"Ask her not to say anything to Grady," I said. "I might have better luck if there's no advance warning."

"Might at that."

It was hot in the barn, dark-shadowed, the air heavy with old smells—hay, manure, dried leather, dust. Two cars were parked in there, a new light blue Geo Storm and an older Ford outfitted with a hand-throttle and a green Handicapped Driver placard on the dash. The Geo was unlocked; I poked around inside, taking my time. Nothing in the glove compartment except the registration, an owner's manual, and a couple of small packets of Kleenex. Nothing on the seats or under the seats except for a lost penny; nothing on or under the floor mats. I pulled the trunk release. Nothing in the trunk that didn't belong there.

I returned to the house. Gus was barking his head off again, but it didn't mean anything; like a lot of people these days, he just liked to hear the sound of his own voice. Haas came out on his crutches, leaving the dog inside, and asked if I'd found anything. I shook my head.

"You figure on coming back here after you talk to Grady?" he asked.

"Not unless there's something we need to discuss. But I'll call you, let you know how it went."

"I'll be here," he said, not without irony. Then he said,

"Tell you something. Last night, lying in bed upstairs, I prayed. Asked God to send that man here so I could put an end to this business myself. You understand? Good Christian and good Catholic all my life and I asked God to let me kill a man."

"I understand. I expect He does too."

"I hope so," Haas said. "Because I ain't sorry. That son of a bitch comes around here, I'll serve him up hot to God or the devil, whichever wants him, and take my own chances when the time comes."

THERE WAS NOT MUCH to the venerable little village of San Lucas. Population: 160. Half a dozen square blocks spread out beyond the no longer used storage silos; red-trimmed country church, post office, red false-fronted grocery store, scattering of stucco-walled houses, a much smaller union school than the one in San Bernado. The place had an aged, south-of-the-border look and feel, as if the whole she-bang had been lifted out of a Sonoran backwater and transplanted here. Even the few people I saw as I drove through might have been natives of Old Mexico.

The Vargas house was on San Benito Street, one of half a dozen side streets that ran at right-angles to the main drag. It was in keeping with the rest of the town: stucco walls, tile roof, sagging wooden fence enclosing a yard dominated by a couple of leafy old shade trees and tangles of prickly pear cactus. Parked on the unpaved street in front was a rust-infested pickup truck and a dusty Chrysler Imperial that had been manufactured during Eisenhower's term of office. I put my car between the two, where it was not at all out of place, and passed through a gate in the tired fence.

Before I got to the front door it opened and disgorged a big, fiftyish woman in a green-and-yellow dress. Constanza Vargas. She had been watching for me, she said in lowered tones. Her eyes were dark and sad, but there was also a kind of hard maternal wariness in them that did not soften until she'd had a good long look at me. She seemed to approve of what she saw. That made two of us.

"Grady is in the backyard," she said, still speaking softly. "She has been there since I brought her this morning."

"Have you tried to talk to her?"

"Yes. She says nothing. She only sits."

"Will you show me where she is?"

She nodded, took my arm and led me around the far side of the house. The rear yard was a larger replica of the front one: three shade trees instead of two, a small vegetable garden to go with more tangles of prickly pear. Under one of the trees was some weathered outdoor furniture, and on one of the chairs was Grady Haas. Not doing anything, just sitting there motionless, hands loose on her lap, jeans-clad legs crossed at the knees. She looked over at us as we approached but without reaction or interest; looked away again before we reached her.

Seeing her up close, in the flesh, was like receiving a low-voltage shock. Except for the fact that she was very pale and wore no makeup of any kind, she looked as she had in the two-year-old photograph in her father's house—same long, lustrous, blue-black hair, same small mouth and high cheekbones and long, slender body; same remote, solemn expression. Yet there was a subtle, alarming difference: something was missing. At first I couldn't quite define what it was. Then, abruptly, I knew.

She wasn't there. Her body sat in the chair, yes; it would get up eventually and walk around and eat and perform its natural functions. But she wasn't inside it. Clone, pod creature, victim of a botched lobotomy . . . no. An empty shell, like a snail's after the snail is gone. Grady Haas didn't live there anymore.

Constanza Vargas said, "Grady, *querida,* this man would like to talk to you."

"All right," she said. The words had the same nonhuman quality as a computer's simulated speech.

Mrs. Vargas glanced at me; her eyes asked if I wanted to be

alone with Grady. I nodded, and she turned immediately and moved away. But not far. Just into the shade of another tree, to wait and watch.

I said, "Grady, I'm—" but she didn't let me finish.

"I know who you are," she said. "The detective my father hired."

"That's right."

"I wish he hadn't."

"He only wants to help you. So do I."

"I don't need any help."

"Everybody needs help sometimes."

"I just want to be left alone."

"Why?"

"It's better that way."

"Better for you, maybe. What about your father?"

"I'm sorry he's so upset, but there's nothing he can do for me or I can do for him. There's nothing anybody can do."

"What happened last Thursday night, Grady? What made you leave San Francisco so suddenly?"

Blank stare—not at me, not at anything in the yard.

"Why did you come home if you didn't want to upset your father? Why not just go somewhere by yourself?"

"That's what I should have done. But I wasn't thinking . . . I got in the car and started driving and this is where I came."

"Why weren't you thinking?"

Headshake.

"Tell me about the man you met on April Fools' Day."

She didn't move, didn't speak.

"Grady?"

"It doesn't matter," she said.

"It matters to me. And to Todd Bellin. He beat up Todd pretty badly, almost broke his neck."

". . . I'm sorry."

"Is that all you have to say?"

"What do you want me to say?"

"He beat up Todd because he thought Todd might know where to find you. That tells me he wants to hurt you too."

"I don't care," she said.

"Why don't you care?"

"He can't hurt me any more than he already has."

"How did he hurt you?"

Headshake.

"What did he do to you, Grady?"

Headshake.

"Who is he? Tell me his name."

A ghastly fleeting smile warped her mouth; a laughing sound came out of her that made my skin crawl. "I don't know his name," she said. "It doesn't matter anyway."

"You don't know it? You mean he gave you a false name?"

No answer.

"Was it David Jones?"

Headshake.

"Then tell me what it was."

No answer.

"All right," I said. "Think about this: Suppose he finds you before I find him? Suppose he harms Mrs. Vargas or her husband? Suppose he harms your father?"

"Why would he do that? It's me he wants."

"They'd try to stop him from getting to you, don't you realize that?"

Silence.

"You want that on your conscience, Grady? Somebody else hurt on account of you?"

". . . No."

"Then keep it from happening. Tell me who the man is, why he's after you, where I can find him."

"He . . . I don't know where he is. Not now."

"Where was he when you were seeing him? Where did he live?"

Headshake.

"In San Francisco? Where?"

"I don't want to talk about him," she said.

"Ostrich," I said, and I had to work to keep the rising anger out of my voice. "Bury your head in the sand and somebody else *will* get hurt. Count on it."

"No. He won't come here."

"How do you know he won't?"

"He doesn't know I come from San Bernado."

"He'll find out. He found Todd Bellin, didn't he?"

"He won't find out. No one in the city knows, not even Todd. There's no way for him to find out."

"So here you sit," I said, "all alone."

"I've always been alone."

"You don't have to be."

The blank stare.

"For how long, Grady? Days, weeks, just sitting or walking in the hills, feeling sorry for yourself? What about your job, your apartment? You can't go back to them as long as this man is on the loose."

"Maybe I should," she said. "Go back to the city."

"And let him find you?"

"I don't care."

"You care. You *haven't* gone back, so you care."

"I don't. Why can't you just leave me alone?"

"Listen to me. He hurt you somehow—all right. You fell in love with the wrong man and he hurt you bad. That's part of it, isn't it?"

No answer.

"You're not the first person it's happened to," I said, "and you won't be the last. Your life's not over."

"Isn't it?"

"It doesn't have to be. You're young, attractive, intelligent. You can get through this if you—"

"Please," she said, "please leave me alone."

"Grady—"

"No," she said, "I don't want to talk about it anymore. It

doesn't matter what happens to me. Why won't you understand that? It doesn't matter."

It doesn't matter. I don't care. Leave me alone. The lyrics of self-pity, repeated over and over until she believed them without question. The Great Tragedy of Grady Haas—like a one-woman Elizabethan melodrama. I had no patience with it. I understood that she'd been emotionally battered, I had not lost my empathy for her, but coming here, seeing her, listening to her, had changed the shape of my attitude toward Little Miss Lonesome. She had people who cared about her, were putting themselves out to keep her safe—even a stranger like me. And here she sat, torn up inside, yes, but with her pain pulled so tightly around her it was like the tissue of a barren womb. Curled in there waiting for release, not that of rebirth but that of death; wanting to die but lacking the courage and with too much self-involvement to do the job herself. A willing victim, and in this lousy world it was the *un*willing victims who had all my compassion and all my tears. No, by God, I had no patience with it at all.

"Okay," I said, "sure, it doesn't matter and we'll all just leave you alone. That way you can pretend none of us exists either. Just poor ravaged Grady Haas, all alone. No crippled father sick with worry. No Constanza, no Mary Ellen, no friends and no loved ones. You're a solipsist, Grady . . . you know what that is? Somebody who thinks he's the only reality, the only being in the universe—everything else is just a figment of his imagination. Nothing matters but you, nothing exists but you. You want me to leave you alone so damn badly, why don't you just will me out of existence?"

I flung the words at her, as hard as if they were stones, letting all the anger come out with them. I wanted her to react. Deny the accusations, defend herself, tell me to shut up or kiss her ass or go to hell, break down and cry—show *some* sign of life and humanity. But she didn't react. The words bounced off her as if they were made of rubber, not stone, leaving no impression of any kind.

She just sat there.

I stared at her while I put a leash on my temper. She didn't move, didn't look at me. Wasn't there—simply was not there.

There was no reason for me to stay any longer; you can't communicate with a shell. I put my back to her and walked past Constanza Vargas, who watched me with her sad eyes. When I reached the side of the house I stopped briefly to look behind me, even though I knew what I would see.

Grady Haas, the willing victim, just sitting there.

LONG DRIVE HOME, made even longer by replaying images of the time in San Lucas. Wasted day, just as I'd expected. Once I thought: She doesn't care what happens to her, why should I? Why go on losing sleep and busting my hump to save the life of a woman who has convinced herself she's already dead? But it was nothing more than a random thought; I didn't give it any serious consideration.

I was not working for Grady Haas—I was working for her father. And he cared, whether she did or not. And dammit, so did I.

Chapter 10

ONE OF HER POTTED PLANTS was dying.

That was the first thing I noticed when I entered Grady's apartment for the second time, a few minutes before nine on Thursday morning. I still had no leads except possibly her neighbors, people named Voorhees and M. Norman/ C. Tagliozzi, and for the third straight day none of them was around to talk to me. Phantom tenants, for Christ's sake. So I decided I might as well have another look through Grady's belongings. Could be I'd overlooked something on my first visit.

The dying plant prodded me straight to the kitchen. There was a plastic watering can on the windowsill; I filled it, watered the wilted plant and all the others in the apartment. Symbolic act, maybe: If her plants lived, flourished again, it was possible that she would, too, in spite of the state she was in now. Or maybe it was just that I'm not the kind of man who can let anything die when it might still be saved.

The place had a different feel to me today than on Tuesday. All the flower patterns and stuffed toys and wicker baskets and pastel colors . . . the aggregate effect seemed frivolous, self-indulgent, not quite real or healthy. It made me uncomfortable. I'd seen Grady through different eyes yesterday; now, as a result, I was seeing her home the same way. And I had no more patience with it and its trappings than I'd had with her.

I started this time with her desk, making myself scan each bill, each credit-card receipt. There was nothing illuminating in any of it—she bought conventional items, from conventional outlets. The only thing of even minor interest was a "Men's Accessories" purchase on her most recent Macy's bill, dated twelve days ago.

I scoured the rest of the living room, then did the same with the dining area, kitchen, bathroom. I learned that Grady had four sets of flowered place mats and two lace tablecloths, and that she liked Grape-Nuts cereal and albacore tuna packed in water and Coffee-mate nondairy creamer, and that she brushed her teeth with Pepsodent and preferred Tylenol to regular aspirin and used Summer's Eve feminine hygiene spray. That was all I learned.

Bedroom. I sifted through the files in the box on the closet floor, again examining each piece of paper in turn. Waste of time; the big trouble in her life went back three weeks, not two years. The remainder of the closet contained clothing, shoes, sweaters stored in plastic boxes—nothing else. The dresser drawers told me she was fond of percale sheets and satin nighties and panties trimmed in lace. I hauled the dresser out from the wall and peered behind it; there wasn't even any dust back there. I looked more closely at the books in the bookcase. Then I got down on one knee and checked under the bed, even though I'd done that on Tuesday. No dust under there either.

I laid my left hand on the nightstand, the way you do to boost yourself up from a kneeling position. Did it automatically, without paying much attention to where the hand went —and my fingers bumped against the hardcover copy of *California Gold,* dislodged it onto the carpet. The book landed on the upper corner of its spine, so that the pages fanned open and the duck-shaped bookmark fell out. When I reached to pick them both up I saw that there was writing on the book-mark, on the bottom part that had been hidden inside.

Sunbrown. Un./Webs. 6:30.

It meant nothing to me. The writing was Grady's, the same as on the cancelled checks in her file—in this case the hurried sort that people use when they're jotting down infor-mation given over the phone.

I took the bookmark into the living room, got her copy of the telephone directory out of the desk. There was one Sun-brown listed—Sunbrown Tanning Salon. The address was 2297 Webster, which would put it near Union Street. *Un./Webs.* . . . Union and Webster.

Grady Haas and a tanning salon? I remembered how pale she'd been yesterday, the whiteness of her arms and ankles. And she was hardly the narcissistic type of woman who goes in for artificial tanning; it would serve to call attention to her, when she had structured her life to avoid attention.

Her mystery man, then? A telephone call, an arrangement to meet at a certain place at a certain time . . . who else? She didn't have any casual friends, and a business meeting seemed unlikely, given the location and the nature of her job.

As I pocketed the bookmark, sounds came filtering in from the lobby—the entrance door thumping shut, footfalls echoing faintly on the tile floor. I stood tight and still, listen-ing.

Whoever it was wasn't coming here; he or she was on the stairs now, going up. I went to the door, eased it open a crack when I could no longer hear the footsteps. Upstairs some-where, another door banged shut. I stepped into the lobby, made sure the lock was engaged, then walked soft out into the vestibule.

The first bell I tried was Norman/Tagliozzi; no answer. I thumbed the one for the Voorhees apartment, and pretty soon the intercom clicked open and a woman's voice said, "Yes? Who is it?"

I gave my name and profession and said that I'd like to talk to her about Grady Haas. There was a pause; then the voice asked, guardedly, if it was important. I said it was. She said, "All right, I'll be down in a minute. I have to go out again anyway."

I waited four minutes, leaning against the vestibule wall with my wallet in my hand. She came down quietly, so that I saw her through one of the heavy glass panels flanking the door before I heard her. She didn't open the door right away, either; she peered out at me, taking my measure, the way smart urban dwellers do these days with unexpected and un-known callers—in particular, smart young female urban dwellers who know, or have a pretty good idea, that they're alone in a building. I smiled to reassure her, held up my open wallet so that she could see the Photostat of my license. Fi-nally she opened the door, but just far enough to slide herself through; and she drew it shut quickly behind her.

She was about twenty-two, blond, of serious mien; lean and narrow in beige slacks and a bulky green sweater. In her left hand she carried a couple of books, one of which was a college text on medical jurisprudence. Her right hand was on the catch of her purse, and I'd have been willing to bet that she had a can of mace inside and that she was as fast on the draw as a Hollywood gunslinger. She moved over to stand with one foot on the sidewalk, her eyes still wary even though I stayed where I was. There was nothing personal in her ultracautious attitude, but it made me feel the way I had in the San Bernado Union School: like a dirty old man.

"Something about Grady Haas, you said?"

"That's right, yes. You're Ms. Voorhees?"

"Christine Voorhees. Missus."

I gave her the same story I'd used on Lisa Fisher—the missing heir possibly entitled to an unspecified sum of money. It didn't impress her much. She shrugged, tucked a stray wisp of hair under the little toque she wore, and shrugged again.

"Well, I don't know what I can tell you," she said. "I don't know her very well. In fact, I hardly know her at all."

"Have you and your husband lived here long?"

"Three years. But between us I'll bet we haven't spoken a hundred words to Grady Haas in all that time."

"She keeps to herself, as I understand it."

"Does she ever."

"So you're not acquainted with any of her friends?"

"For all I know she doesn't have any friends."

"Does that include men as well as women?"

Another shrug.

"I've been told she has a new male friend," I said, "a man she met within the past few weeks. But I can't seem to find out who he is."

"Well, I'm sure I don't know."

"I don't even have a good description of him. You wouldn't happen to have seen her with a man during the past three weeks, would you?"

". . . As a matter of fact, I did."

"When was that?"

"Oh, about two weeks ago. A Saturday night. Tom and I . . . Tom's my husband . . . we were coming home from dinner and Grady Haas and this man were just going into her apartment."

"Did you get a good look at him?"

"I only saw him for a few seconds. She pulled him inside as if she was afraid we might take him away from her."

"Can you describe him?"

"Well, he was good-looking. I remember being surprised she could attract such a hunk. I always thought she was . . . you know, that she didn't much care for men. Tom said maybe it was business or something, but it didn't look like business to me. Not the way she was holding on to his arm."

"Big, was he?"

"Heavyset, broad shoulders. Not too tall, though."

"Under six feet?"

"Tom's five-eleven. About that."

"How old, would you say?"

"I don't know . . . thirty-five or so."

"What color hair?"

"Brown. Dark brown."

"Straight, wavy, curly?"

"Straight."

"Cut short or long?"

"Short. Not a flattop, just a regular cut."

"Did you notice the color of his eyes?"

"No. The light isn't very good in the lobby."

"Is there anything else about him you can remember?"

"Well . . . he had a nice tan."

"Did he."

"Like he'd just come back from Hawaii."

Or spent some time in a tanning salon.

"He had a scar too," Christine Voorhees said. "A little one under his eye. I saw that all right because it stood out against his tan."

"Which side of his face?"

"Um . . . the right side. Under his right eye."

"About how long was the scar?"

"An inch or so. Just a small one."

"Straight or jagged?"

"Curved, like a . . . what's that sword the Arabs have?"

"Scimitar?"

"Right. Like a scimitar."

"Did the man say anything to you or your husband?"

"No. She didn't give him time."

"And you haven't seen again since that night?"

"No."

"Do you remember the last time you saw Grady Haas?"

"Not really. Last week sometime."

"Last Thursday night, by any chance?"

"Thursday night? No, I don't think so. Tom and I stay home on Thursdays to watch *L.A. Law.*"

"Early Friday morning, then?"

"No, I don't think so."

"Did anything unusual happen last Thursday night or Friday morning?"

"Unusual?"

"Here in your building or in the neighborhood."

"I'm not sure I know what you mean by unusual."

"Loud arguments, unexplained noises—anything out of the ordinary."

"No. Why do you want to know that?"

I said something vague about covering all the bases. "Would you know if Grady Haas was home Thursday night? Hear her moving around, see her lights on?"

"We live on the third floor and I got home before dark." Christine Voorhees had relaxed during the course of our conversation, to the point where now she was bored with it and with me. She glanced at her watch. "I really have to be going or I'll be late for my next class. There's nothing else I can tell you."

"You've been very helpful, Mrs. Voorhees."

"Have I? Good," she said, without meaning it.

I watched her walk away. The new breed. Excellent student, probably, and someday she'd be the kind of lawyer who had all the fine points of the law honed sharp. But I wouldn't want her working for me. There wasn't much humanity in Christine Voorhees. She and others of her generation were like the machines they had learned to rely on: highly competent, coldly logical, utterly humorless, and about as emotional as a microchip. The world they were inheriting may be badly flawed, but it wasn't half as bleak, to my way of thinking, as the one they were going to help reshape.

UNION STREET LIES between Pacific Heights, where I've lived for thirty years thanks to a landlord who has yet to give in to the Heights' now-exorbitant rental prices, and Cow Hollow and the Marina, which were so heavily damaged in the October quake that repairs are still going on. One of the city's trendy streets, Union; has been for years. Antiques shops, art galleries, boutiques, new and antique jewelry stores, and chic restaurants have taken it over from Van Ness to Fillmore, though they haven't yet squeezed out such venerable fixtures as Perry's watering hole, the Metro Theatre, and Solar Lights Books. A tanning salon, one of the few eighties fads that had yet to die out, was a perfect fit. So perfect that Sunbrown almost certainly wasn't the only one in the neighborhood.

It was just down from the north corner of Union and Webster. And it was closed, which wasn't surprising; Union Street businesses tend to open late and stay open until seven or eight o'clock, to catch the evening trade. I parked in a yellow zone long enough to go over and look at the sign on the salon's front. SAFE, GOLDEN TANS, it said. FDA APPROVED. WOLFF AND SILVER UVA TANNING SENSORS. PRIVATE ROOMS, AM/FM STEREO SYSTEM. OPEN 11 AM–11 PM DAILY. It was now just ten o'clock.

My office was only about a mile away; I went there instead of hanging around Union. No business. And for the third day in a row, no sign of Eberhardt. Annoyed, I called his home number and got the machine again. This time I left a message: "We need to talk. And there's work that needs to be done. Get your ass down to the office or at least let me know you're still alive."

The mail came while I was making up a deposit slip to go with Arlo Haas's check. In one envelope was a check from a skip-trace client I'd been dunning for four months and last week had threatened with a mail-fraud claim. There's nothing like the threat of mail fraud to make a deadbeat reach for his wallet; everybody is afraid of the feds and that goes double for people like my ex-client, who use the mails as part of whatever services they render. I added his check to the deposit slip, and when I toted up the new balance in the agency account I was pleasantly surprised.

Maybe my luck was changing. Maybe this was going to turn out to be a decent day after all.

Chapter **11**

THE WOMAN BEHIND the reception desk in Sunbrown's sunbrown anteroom was halfway through her twenties, cornsilk blond and sunbrown as a nut. She was so sunbrown and so healthy-looking, in fact, that I felt pale and sickly, not to mention old, in comparison. She laid aside the paperback she'd been reading—*Passion's Sweet Hurricane,* by one Jennifer Javier—and showed me a smile that would have dazzled the Cheshire cat. If an ad exec for a toothpaste company ever got a look at that smile and the teeth that went with it, he'd have her under contract in ten minutes flat.

"May I help you, sir?"

"Well, I don't know," I said. I put a worried note into my voice and a worried expression on my face. "I'm trying to find my daughter and I . . . well, the man she ran off with is a customer of yours. At least I *think* he's a customer of yours. I really don't know much about him, you see, not even his name. . . ." I stopped and cleared my throat before I went on. "I'm sorry, I didn't mean to babble at you like that. It's just that I'm worried about my little girl. She's only eighteen and I'm afraid he . . . well, that he doesn't really love her, if you know what I mean."

The sunbrown blonde's smile had disappeared; in its place was a look of sympathy mixed with a touch of avid interest. Readers of historical romance novels tend to be a compassionate lot, especially when there's a peg of soap-opera sex, pathos, and intrigue to hang their compassion on.

"I know what you mean," she said. "Do I ever. I'd be worried, too, if my daughter ran off with some guy when she's eighteen."

"You have a daughter?"

"She's three. Her name's Candy Two."

"Too?"

"The number two. I'm Candy One."

"Oh, I see."

"What's her name? Your daughter?"

"Grady," I said. "Grady Haas."

It didn't mean anything to her. She said, "The guy she ran off with . . . you don't know his name?"

"Grady called him Buck, but that's not his real name. I've seen a picture of him, though; she's got one in her room at home. I guess I should have brought it along. . . ."

"Well, what does he look like? I know most of our customers; I probably know him."

"He's about thirty-five, not too tall, heavyset, broad shoulders, short brown hair. And he has a little curved scar under his right eye."

"Oh," she said, "Jack King."

"Jack King."

"Sure. That must be why he didn't come in on Monday."

"He had an appointment this past Monday?"

"Monday afternoon, but he didn't show up. I guess it was because he ran off with your daughter."

"Has he been a customer long?"

"Not long. A month or so. Just since he came here."

"Here?"

"To the city."

"He's only been in San Francisco a month or so?"

"That's what he said."

"Where did he come from?"

"Back East someplace. Maybe New York."

"What makes you think that?"

"Well, he's got that kind of accent."

"Brooklyn? The Bronx?"

"New York," she said.

"Would you have any idea where he lives?"

"You mean in New York?"

"No. Here in the city."

"Sure. We have his address."

"Ah," I said.

"All our customers have to fill out a form," Candy One said. "That's so we can send them literature and stuff, like when we're having specials or when we get in some new equipment."

"Would you mind looking it up for me?"

"Jack King's address?"

"Yes," I said patiently, "Jack King's address."

"We're not supposed to give out personal information. . . ."

"If it was your daughter, I'd do it for you."

". . . Oh, hell, all right. I'll be right back."

She went away through a door behind the desk. Jack King, I thought. It sounded like another phony—two playing cards, jack and king—but it didn't have to be. Depended on who and what he was, if there was any reason for him not to provide his real name, as there'd been when he called Intercoastal asking for information about Grady. The same was true of his real local address.

Candy One brought a piece of paper back with her. I favored her with my best forlorn look, added a sigh, and held out my hand—and she let me have the paper without objection or hesitation. Sunbrown Customer Questionnaire, with not much filled out on it. The name Jack King, printed in a bold hand. Broadmoor Hotel, San Francisco. Occupation: salesman. The other spaces on the form he'd left blank.

I said, "So he's a salesman. Do you know what he sells?"

"No, I don't think he ever said."

"Maybe he mentioned it to another employee."

"I can ask Bud. He works the machines and does massage."

"Please. And ask him if King mentioned where he was from or anything else about himself."

She went away again, and this time when she came back it was with nothing for me. "Bud says he and Jack King hardly talked at all. Mr. King just went in and got into bed and that's it."

"Bed, did you say?"

She laughed. "One of our tanning beds. You didn't think I meant with *Bud,* did you?"

THE BROADMOOR WAS one of the city's older hotels, having risen like a latter-day phoenix from the ashes and rubble of the 1906 quake. It was on Sutter, a few blocks uphill from Union Square, and catered to businessmen and tourists who preferred a lodging place that was small, quiet, not too expensive, and within walking distance of the downtown attractions. Respectable was the word for it, with a Victorian flavor that had been enhanced by a complete remodeling a few years back. If Jack King *had* been living there for a month or so, it meant that he or the company he worked for—if he worked for a company—had money and taste. You won't find the Broadmoor in most puff literature about the city's hostelries.

The lobby was pillared, darkly appointed, and empty when I walked in out of another blustery afternoon. The youngish desk clerk wore a bow tie and an expression that straddled the line between servility and snootiness. He gave me the once-over, to make sure I wasn't one of the homeless people who wandered the streets even up here, and decided to step over into his servile mode. But only a short step; I wasn't the sort of moneyed type who commanded total deference.

I asked him if a Mr. Jack King was registered. He said, "I don't believe so, sir," and consulted a register or file that was hidden from me by the countertop. "No, Mr. King is no longer with us."

"When did he check out?"

"Last Saturday."

"Did he leave a forwarding address?"

Another under-the-counter consultation. "No, sir."

"He was here about a month, is that right?"

"Five weeks, to be exact."

"Would you happen to know if he was in the city on business?"

"I couldn't say, sir."

"His home town is New York, though, isn't it?"

The clerk's mouth got puckery, as if he'd just bitten down on a persimmon cough drop; his snooty mode was the one he preferred and he seemed almost relieved to step back into it. "I'm sorry," he lied, omitting the "sir" this time, "I really can't provide personal information about our guests." After which he pointedly turned his back, dismissing me.

I was on my way out, taking my time about it, when one of two elevators disgorged a uniformed bell captain. The desk clerk still had his back to the lobby, so I detoured over and braced the captain. He was my age, just as worn around the edges, and inclined to be cooperative, especially after I steered him behind a pillar and gave him the same worried-father pitch I'd given to Candy One. His name, according to a little brass plate on the front of his jacket, was Harvey.

"Sure, I remember Mr. King," he said. "Kept to himself pretty much, but he seemed like a decent guy."

"I understand he's a salesman. He happen to mention what it is he sells?"

"Not to me."

"Or what company he's with?"

"No. Might be on his registration card, though, if he took the corporate rate. Probably did, since he was here so long."

"Do you know if he had a car?"

"I believe he did."

"His own or a rental?"

"You got me there."

"Make and model?"

"Can't tell you that either."

"Broadmoor doesn't have a hotel garage, does it?"

"No. Likely he kept it up at Milton's Garage on the next block. We have an arrangement with them to validate parking for our guests."

"I'll check with them. Would you have any idea if King had a preference for any café or restaurant or bar in the area?"

Harvey shook his head. "Sid might know," he said. "He's the night captain."

"What time does he come on?"

"Six. I could ask him for you." He lowered his voice another couple of octaves, even though we were already speaking softly. "I can check the registration card, too, see if Mr. King's home address or company name is on it. Dawson, the desk clerk, won't tell you one way or the other; he thinks he owns the place."

"I know," I said, "I've already talked to him. One other thing you might do, if there's no home address and if King paid his bill by credit card: write the card number down for me. I might be able to trace him through that."

"Okay. And I'll ask Sid if he knows anything about Mr. King that might help you."

I gave Harvey twenty dollars to show him how much I appreciated his help. I also gave him my home phone number. He said he'd call as soon as he had anything to tell me and I believed him. He had an honest face. Besides, it was a good idea for me to maintain a certain amount of faith in my fellow man; I was cynical enough as it was.

* * *

TWO PARKING ATTENDANTS were on duty at Milton's Garage. One of them remembered Jack King; the other one looked as though he might have difficulty remembering his own name and where he lived. The brighter one said he thought King's car was a Buick, dark brown, and that it was a rental. But he couldn't remember the name of the rental company. And he couldn't tell me anything else about King.

THERE WERE HALF A DOZEN coffee shops and taverns within a two-block radius of the Broadmoor. I made the rounds of them, describing Jack King to waitresses and bartenders and patrons. Nobody owned up to having had a conversation with him or even to having laid eyes on him in the past five weeks.

I lingered in the last of the coffee shops long enough to eat a bowl of soup and some crackers and to use the restroom. On the wall above the urinal was some pseudointellectual graffiti: "Great minds write about ideas. Average minds write about things. Small minds write about people." Under that, in a different hand, somebody had added a fourth statement that was both ironic and more profound than the other three.

"Assholes write on walls."

ON THE WAY BACK to my car, struggling against what had evolved into a chilly twenty-knot wind, I had a minor altercation with a shabbily dressed white panhandler whose hair was so knotted and greasy it was like a mockery of a black man's dreadlocks. He wanted a dollar and he didn't ask for it politely; he got right up in my face so that I had a sickening whiff of body odor, bad breath, and cheap wine, and demanded it in an or-else voice.

I took him for one of the derelict substance-abusers and borderline thugs that roam the city these days, making the plight of the genuine homeless even more difficult. You can't always tell the real thing from the phony, though. There is plenty of anger and aggression among the homeless, too; and some of them, out of shame and bitterness and frustration, let themselves go to seed and take to liquor and drugs. I have compassion for anybody who is forced by circumstances to live on the streets, but I draw the line at threatening behavior, no matter the cause. You see more and more of this type of hard-ass panhandling in the city, and too often it results in violence. The mean streets, as far as I'm concerned, are too damned mean already.

I told this guy to back off; he didn't do it. So we played stare-down for ten seconds or so. He lost, as he'd have lost any other game he might have tried to play with me. We both got off lucky, because that was as far as it went. He told me to go fuck myself, not quite as belligerently as he'd demanded the dollar, and the wind blew him away.

Assholes writing on walls, assholes roaming the streets, assholes everywhere you looked, in all shapes and sizes and intellects and economic situations. Next thing you knew, they'd form a union and their own political party and then the country would *really* be in trouble.

AT THE OFFICE I spent close to an hour on the phone checking car-rental agencies large and small. Nobody named Jack King or David Jones from New York or anywhere else had taken a long-term rental on a dark brown Buick within the past two months. Which meant one of three things: he'd rented the Buick in some other state and driven it to California; he owned the car and the attendant at Milton's had been mistaken; his name *wasn't* Jack King and he'd rented it under his real name or a different alias. In any of those cases, I was smack up against another dead-end.

The day was going downhill again. And the fact that Eberhardt still hadn't put in an appearance, or returned my earlier call, wasn't helping matters. Every time I glanced at his empty desk, with its unanswered messages and piled-up caseload, I got a little hotter under the collar. At four-thirty, after the tenth straight negative on the car-rental angle, I decided I'd had enough.

I closed up, went and got my car, and pointed it toward Noe Valley. Eb and I were going to get this wedding business and his selfish unprofessionalism settled today. Yes we were— one way or another.

Chapter **12**

HE WAS HOME, all right. He'd converted his garage into a workshop a while back, cramming it so full of woodworking equipment that he had to leave his car in the driveway or on the street; it was in the driveway today, canted at an off-angle that told me he'd driven it up over the curb. It also told me he hadn't been out of the house all day and that when he'd come home—last night, probably—he'd been potted. That made me even angrier. Drinking and driving, the damn fool. What if he'd hurt somebody?

I rang the bell, working it hard. No answer. I punched the bell some more, banged on the door and yelled his name, and still he didn't come. By then I was steaming. I went down off the porch, into what he laughably referred to as his garden, and got the spare key he kept under one of the decorative lava rocks and then went back up and let myself in.

He was lying on the couch in the darkened living room, shoes off and a blanket over his big frame. When I walked in there he hoisted himself onto one elbow and fixed me with a bleary-eyed glare. The room stank of the lousy pipe tobacco he smoked; he stank of bar whiskey and self-pity. I could smell him from ten feet away and I didn't want to get any closer.

"What the hell's the big idea?" he said.

"I got the same question for you. What's the big idea not answering the bell? You knew it was me."

"I don't want to talk to you. I don't want to talk to anybody right now."

"Yeah," I said. "Two days now. How many more?"

He was deaf to that. He said, "I don't like you walking in here uninvited. You hear me?"

"I hear you. But I thought maybe you were dead. It's too bad you're not." I flipped the switch for the overhead light. He grimaced when it came on, made a pained noise and threw an arm up over his eyes like a vampire confronted with sunlight. His face was gray, beard-stubbled; if his eyes were any indication he was bleeding internally. "You look like hell," I said. "Two-day drunks look like seven-day drunks on you."

"Get out of here," he said. "Leave me alone."

Leave me alone. It doesn't matter. I don't care. An older, male version of Grady Haas. Another damn willing victim.

"Self-pity taste good, does it?" I asked him.

"Self-pity, my ass."

"You got another name for it?"

"You come here to rub my nose in it?"

"No."

"Then what the hell you want?"

"Why haven't you been to the office? Or at least been in touch?"

"Oh for Chrissake. I'm sick, can't you see that?"

"Sick, yeah. From being pig drunk two nights in a row."

". . . I got a right. You think I don't?"

"You got a right to drive drunk too?"

"A few blocks, that's all," he said defensively. "I was down at the Shamrock on Twenty-fourth, I closed the place, it was two A.M.—"

"I don't care where you were or how late it was. You could've killed somebody."

"All right, all right, I screwed up—"

"Man, you can say that again. In spades."

"Don't start on me."

"No? Why not? Somebody's got to lay it on the line and it might as well be me."

"I'm not gonna listen to you—"

"Yes you are. You're the one who bitched up the wedding, not Bobbie Jean. You and your fancy plans. Wedding cakes, musicians, limos to the airport . . . Jesus! It's a wonder she didn't call it off a lot sooner."

"You smug bastard, you think you know so much."

"I know a horse's ass when I see one."

He struggled into a sitting position. His jowly face was mottled red now, to match his eyes. "I don't have to listen to that crap in my own house. Who you think you are?"

"Your friend and your partner. Which is more than *you* can say right now."

"What's that supposed to mean?"

"You haven't done enough work the past month to draw half pay," I said. "Your desk's piled high with unfinished business. I've spent half my time either doing your work or covering your ass."

"Oh fine, fine, now I get a guilt trip laid on me. On top of everything else I got to put up with . . ."

He hauled himself to his feet, put his back to me and walked unsteadily through the dining room into the kitchen. I went after him, watched him yank open the refrigerator and haul out a half-full carton of orange juice. He drank thirstily with his head tilted back—spilling some of it onto his bathrobe, making slurping noises that set my teeth on edge. I used to think I was a slob; he was a hell of a lot worse.

I said, "When are you going to grow up, accept responsibility for your own actions?"

He put the orange juice carton back into the fridge, even

though it was empty, and slammed the door. Without looking at me he said, "You still here?"

"Yeah, I'm still here. Well?"

"Well what?"

"When are you going to accept responsibility?"

"For what?"

"For your own actions, goddamn it. For your mistakes."

"It's all my fault, huh? *All* of it."

"Well isn't it?"

"No!"

"Call Bobbie Jean," I said.

". . . What?"

"You heard me. Call Bobbie Jean, apologize to her before it's too late."

"I got nothing to apologize for. Let her call me."

"She won't. She's the one with nothing to apologize for."

"That's right, keep on taking her side."

"I'm not taking sides here, I'm trying to talk some sense into that thick head of yours. Bobbie Jean loves you, she's the best thing that's ever happened to you, don't throw her away because your pride is hurt."

"Me throw her away? Me? *I'm* not the one called off the frigging marriage."

"She didn't call off the marriage, she called off the wedding. There's a big difference."

"Not from where I sit."

"So you won't apologize to her?"

"No. The hell with her."

"You don't mean that, Eb."

"I mean it, all right. I put two thousand bucks into that wedding, I wanted it to be perfect for her and she threw it all back in my face. How you think I feel, huh? Everybody laughing at me, feeling sorry for me—"

"Nobody's laughing at you or feeling sorry for you."

"—all my so-called friends, and why? Because *she* decides at the last minute she can't put up with the pomp and circumstance. That's what she said, pomp and circumstance . . . two thousand dollars worth of pomp and circumstance. Well, the hell with her."

"Mr. Wonderful," I said. "I thought you loved her."

"Not anymore I don't."

"Don't like me too much either, huh?"

"You got that right."

"So what're you going to do? Quit the agency, withdraw from the human race? Get drunk every night and lie around here every day feeling sorry for yourself?"

"Big man," he said. "Smart guy. Knows what's best for everybody except himself."

I had nothing to say to that.

Eberhardt said, "You think your head's screwed on so damn tight these days? Not since that kidnap business, it hasn't been."

"Don't bring that up," I said, hard and tight. "We're not talking about that."

"Why the hell not? You come into my house and dump shit all over me, now it's my turn. This past year you been hard to get along with and reckless as hell, busting laws left and right, putting both our licenses in jeopardy. Look at the Lujack case, look at all the harebrained crap you pulled—"

"Eb, shut up." I could feel myself starting to shake inside.

"Can't take it, huh? Dish it out but can't take it. Maybe you ought to go see a head doctor, buddy boy. You ever consider that, you self-righteous pain in the ass?"

"Back off. I've had enough of this."

"So have I. You think I haven't?"

"Then back off."

"No, *you* back off. Get the hell out of my house." A vein bulged and pulsed in his neck. "I'm not gonna tell you again."

"Suppose I don't want to leave? You going to throw me out?"

"If that's the way you want it."

"You can try," I said.

His eyes got flinty and he took a couple of steps toward me —close enough so that I could smell the stale-whiskey sourness of his breath. "Don't push me anymore," he said, "I'm warning you."

"You mean like this?" I poked his shoulder with the heel of my hand, hard enough to force him backward a step.

He growled something and came back at me in a bullish rush. But hangover had dulled his reflexes; the punch he threw was slow and I had no trouble avoiding it. I didn't think, didn't hesitate. I hit him once in the belly, short-arming the blow but not pulling it any. The air went hissing out of him. He staggered backward, folding at the middle; smacked into the drainboard and then sat down hard enough on the floor to rattle dishes inside the cupboards.

All the anger went out of me as swiftly as the air had gone out of Eberhardt. It left me feeling shocked, muddleheaded, a little sick. Neither of us moved for a little time; just stood and sat staring at each other in disbelief. Then, jerkily, I started toward him.

"Eb . . ."

"Stay away from me, you son of a bitch."

I'd put my hand out; he batted it away. His face had gone gray again and he was clutching at his belly. He used his other hand to clutch the edge of the sink, lift himself upright. When he was on his feet I saw his stomach convulse, heard the sickness bubbling in his throat. He spun away from me, lurching, and banged out of the kitchen and through the house to the downstairs bathroom.

I could hear him vomiting in there. I wanted to go to him, say something, tell him I was sorry, try to erase what had just happened between us, but I couldn't seem to move—not until the puking sounds stopped and I heard the splash of running water. Then I was able to make my legs work, but I didn't go to where he was. I went straight to the front door and out and down to my car.

I sat there. Feeling lousy, disgusted with myself. Ashamed.

My hand hurt a little—the knuckles on the ring and little fingers, where they'd scraped against his rib cage. I looked at the hand but there wasn't any damage; just a faint quivering, as if something was causing it to vibrate internally. There was something clenched in my other hand, I realized then. His spare key. I looked at that, too, then got out of the car and went up and replaced it under the lava rock.

In the car again I remembered the one other time we'd fought: thirty years ago, at the police academy just a few weeks after we met. One of those cases of instant dislike between two people that forms for no good reason and builds out of nothing much into a confrontation: harsh words, an exchange of blows. I'd knocked him down then too. Right hook to the side of the head. And my hand had hurt afterward just as it was hurting now.

Kid stuff.

But in the funny way of things, that fight had made us friends. Friends for three full decades, partners for the last five years. Plenty of disagreements and crises large and small, plenty of *words,* but in all that time we had never again come to blows. Until today.

Why?

Over what, really?

My fault. I could have prevented it; instead I'd provoked it by shoving him. Why had I shoved him like that?

Willing victim . . . surrogate for Grady Haas?

Maybe you ought to go see a head doctor, buddy boy.

Ah Jesus, I thought.

Then I thought: It'll be all right, it's just a thing that happened. He already feels as bad about it as I do. A few days, at most a week, and it'll blow over. No permanent damage to our friendship; I'll see to that. Someday we'll laugh about it, same as we laugh about the time at the police academy.

I didn't believe it.

Chapter **13**

I DROVE AROUND for a while, trying to work myself out of depression and a dull self-hatred. The aimless vehicular wandering didn't do much good; I kept right on not liking myself.

When night began to fold down I went home. I opened the refrigerator first thing, but I was on automatic pilot: I had no appetite nor even any desire for a beer. In the bathroom I washed my face with cold water and took another look at my hand. It still hurt, or maybe I was just imagining that it hurt. Guilt creates all sorts of little phantoms.

I sat on the bed, looked at the phone. I wanted to call Eberhardt, but even if he answered—and chances were he wouldn't—he would just hang up when he heard my voice. And what would I say to him anyway? "I'm sorry" wouldn't cut it, and I couldn't think of anything else worthwhile.

I felt, too, that I ought to call Bobbie Jean, tell her what had taken place. Or Kerry; Kerry would understand. But I just sat there. Truth was, I did not want to talk about what had happened between Eberhardt and me. Not tonight, not until the edge of shame dulled away and I quit feeling bad about myself.

I'd been staring at the phone for a good three minutes before it registered that the message light on the answering machine was on. Old Eagle Eye. I ran the tape back. One message, from Harvey, the bell captain at the Broadmoor Hotel. He had some things to tell me, he said; I could reach him at home, here's the number, call anytime before eleven.

So I called him, and he said, "I didn't find out much, but maybe there's something that'll help."

"I appreciate it in any case."

"Well, first, I talked to Sid, the night captain. He don't know much about Jack King, either, but he did see him with a woman one night a couple of weeks ago. At the hotel. They were together in the lobby."

"Could he describe the woman?"

"Young, slim, dark. Long wavy black hair. About thirty. That your daughter?"

"No," I said, "but I know her. Was there anything unusual about the meeting, did Sid say?"

"No. Just said he saw them together in the lobby."

"Anything else?"

"One night last week," Harvey said, "Mr. King came down and asked Sid to get him a cab. Sid heard him tell the driver he wanted to go to North Beach."

"Any particular place in North Beach?"

"Panotti's. I think it's a restaurant."

"It is. On upper Grant."

"You been there, then?"

"A couple of times. Not recently."

"Well, that's all Sid knows," Harvey said. "I checked Mr. King's registration card and bill, like I said I would, but he didn't give a home address or telephone number. No forwarding address either."

"He put down a home city?"

"New York. That's all."

"What about the company he works for?"

"No company name. He didn't take the corporate rate."

"And he didn't pay with a credit card, I'll bet."

"Afraid not. Traveler's checks."

"Any notation as to which bank issued them?"

"I couldn't find any," Harvey said.

Panotti's, in North Beach.

All right. At least it was a place to go tonight, something to occupy my time and my mind. The walls here were already starting to close in.

NORTH BEACH IS not what it used to be. Not by a long shot. Like so many things that were once good, worth preserving intact, it has been caught up in the web of mindless change and its vital juices sucked out of it by the spiders of greed and exploitation.

For three-quarters of a century North Beach had been a rock-ribbed Little Italy, built on the slopes of Telegraph Hill by Genovese and Sicilian fishermen in the 1880s. Its decline began in the 1950s—Italian families moving to the suburbs, the expansion of Chinatown and the gobbling up of North Beach real estate by wealthy Chinese, the influx of beatniks and hippies and motorcycle toughs and drug dealers—and as far as I'm concerned the decline is still going on. There has been a small, new wave of immigrants from Italy in recent years, but they are mostly young and upscale; their interests lie more in realizing the American Dream than in preserving what's left of their countrymen's San Francisco heritage. The old North Beach is doomed. Nothing can save it because nothing can stop the accelerated rate of change, the unquenchable lust of modern society for the new, the easy, the *now*. *Sic transit. Requiescat in pace.* Hey, the past is dead and who the hell cares anyway, in the long run?

Parking in the Beach is the worst in the city. On weekends and evenings you can drive around its hilly streets for hours without finding a legal space. Upper Grant, where Panotti's was located, is narrow, traffic-clogged at night, and a parking-space nightmare; I didn't even bother with it. The fringes are where you're more apt to get lucky, and where I finally claimed a semilegal chunk of curb overlapping a corner on Filbert and Mason, eight blocks away. And it took me half an hour of looking to find that.

Panotti's was a narrow storefront near Green, squeezed between an Italian hardware store and the Sip Hing Herb Company. It specialized in Calabrian-Lucanian cooking: baked *maccheroni* with tomatoes, *crocchette di carne arrostite*, spaghetti with squid ink, anchovy dishes such as *tortiera di alici*, and rich, fig-based desserts. Very good, all of it, but on the expensive side. The place was packed on Friday and Saturday nights; on weeknights, especially after nine o'clock, you could get a table without waiting. I could have had one this night, if I'd been there to eat dinner and if my appetite had come back. As it was, the fine spicy aromas from the kitchen made me faintly queasy.

Less than half of the twenty tables were occupied, and there was nobody at the short bar along the left-hand wall as you came in. I went to the bar first. The guy behind it was middle-aged, balding, and solemn; eating and drinking to the Italian is a serious business. I ordered a beer that I didn't want and asked him in Italian how he was this fine evening, to establish the fact that we were *compaesani*. One *'paesano* will tell another what he won't tell anybody else.

But he didn't have anything to tell me. He listened to my heir-hunter pitch, and my description of Jack King, and then shook his head and spread his hands and said he didn't remember anybody who looked like that. Then, because we were *compaesani*, he suggested I go talk to Angelo, the head waiter. Angelo had a good memory for faces, he said.

I waited a couple of minutes for Angelo to come back from the kitchen. He was sixtyish, slender, and very elegant in a black tux and a bow tie. Amenities first, then the pitch and description of King. Angelo frowned, scratched his chin, nibbled at a couple of hairs on his neat little mustache—a ritual, I thought, designed to help with the memory-cudgeling process.

"Oh, sure," he said at length. "I remember him. Last week he come in, Monday . . . no, Tuesday night. For the special that night the chef makes *coniglio alla cacciatore*— you know, the rabbit in wine vinegar—and that's what he have. But his name, it's not King. Jack, could be, but not King."

"How do you know that?"

"I hear his name at the table."

"What name?"

"Blackwell. Sure, Mr. Blackwell."

"You're positive that's what it was?"

"I hear it two, maybe three times," Angelo said. "Big dark hole in the ground, that's how I remember."

"He didn't eat alone then. He was with somebody."

"Sure. He's eat with good customer, comes in all the time."

"You know this customer?"

"Sure. He's *compaesano* too. But Genovese, I think."

"His name, Angelo?"

"Savarese," Angelo said. "Mr. Vernon Savarese."

SO NOW I HAD A CONNECTION, or part of a connection. But just what was it I had?

More questions, a whole new set of them.

Savarese and Blackwell a.k.a. Jack King a.k.a. David Jones—and Grady Haas. It seemed pretty likely now that Grady had met Blackwell at or near Savarese Importing on April Fools' Day; any other explanation, in light of what I'd just learned from Angelo, was stretching coincidence a little too far. Did Savarese know about the meeting, know that Grady and Blackwell had become lovers? If he knew, why had he lied to me about it? What was his relationship with Blackwell? And whatever the relationship, did it have anything to do with why Blackwell was on the hunt for Little Miss Lonesome?

Angelo had no more answers for me. No, he hadn't listened to what Mr. Savarese and Mr. Blackwell were talking about; did I think he was a *spionaggio,* an eavesdropper? No, it was just the two of them having dinner, nobody else. No, they didn't act like friends; if they were friends, Mr. Savarese wouldn't have called him Mr. Blackwell, hah? Sure—business associates, that's how they seemed. No, he hadn't seen Mr. Blackwell since that night. Nor Mr. Savarese. No, he didn't know where Mr. Savarese lived. Somewhere in the city, probably, on account of Mr. Savarese was a good customer, came in once or twice a month, and who's going to drive in from out of town that often, even for fine Calabrian food like you always got at Panotti's?

Angelo's patience was wearing thin by then; I was keeping him from work he loved. I let him get on with it and went to the restroom area, where there was a public telephone and a city directory. But that didn't buy me anything. There was a listing for Savarese Importing but none for Vernon or V. Savarese.

So I would have to put off another talk with him until tomorrow morning, down at his scabrous old warehouse on China Basin Street. In the morning, too, I would call up one of Eberhardt's cronies at the Hall of Justice, give him the Blackwell and King and Jones names and the man's description and possible New York origin, and ask him to run a computer check through the National Crime Information Center, see if maybe they added up to a criminal record and a positive ID.

ONLY I DIDN'T GET to do either of those things as early as I'd planned. Because when I arrived at my office building on Friday morning, I found a nasty little surprise waiting for me.

Chapter **14**

THE FRONT DOOR to the building was unlocked. I might not have paid any attention to that, because the lights were already on in Bay City Realtors; the firm's owner, Martin Quon, was as much an early-bird workaholic as I am. But the latch had an odd, loose feel, and that caused me to look down at it— then take a closer look. That was when I saw the scratches on the plate, the edge of bent metal.

I was on one knee, still looking, when Martin Quon came out of his offices. He was a dapper guy in his thirties, calm on the surface and a dynamo underneath. He said, "I thought you'd notice it right away."

"Yeah."

"Somebody off the street looking for money, I suppose. But he must've been scared off."

"Why do you say that?"

"He didn't get into my offices. Door was still secure. Not that it would have done him any good; you'd have to be crazy to keep cash on the premises overnight in this neighborhood. But the potential damage . . . well, you know what I mean."

I got slowly to my feet. This was a borderline neighborhood, all right, with the Tenderloin and its drug and homeless problems just a few blocks away. Burglaries were common enough in this part of the city, although our building hadn't been hit yet. Still hadn't been hit: This was not your standard street-type B & E. Addicts and bums don't use picks and jimmy bars to bust through a lock, and they don't make the effort to do it in such a way that it might pass undetected.

I asked Martin, "You report this?"

"Not yet. I was only five minutes ahead of you."

"Well, don't. At least not until I check upstairs."

"Not much point in reporting it anyway," he said cynically. "If anything's missing, it's gone for good."

I didn't bother with the elevator; I climbed the fire stairs instead. On the second floor I stopped long enough to check the door to the Slim-Taper Shirt Company. Secure, no signs of disturbance. Tight-drawn, I went on up to the third floor.

The door to my office was locked but that didn't mean it hadn't been breached; the lock on it was the push-button snap kind—a hot prowler's dream. The landlord was a cheap bastard: I'd asked him twice to put in a deadbolt and both times he said he'd think about it and that was the end of that. I could have had one installed at my own expense, but I hadn't gotten around to it. Low priority, or so I'd figured. What was here for anybody to steal except Eberhardt's computer?

I used my key. At first glance everything looked to be as I'd left it yesterday. But there was a wrongness here, a residual aura of violation that I would have felt even if I hadn't been primed by the damaged lock downstairs. I shut the door, made a quick tour of the office and then a more careful one. Nothing obvious missing—I was sure of that. Some papers had been shuffled around on my desk, and the silver-framed photograph of Kerry that I keep there had been moved. The thought of him handling the frame, holding it up and looking at her in the light of a flash beam, drew me even tighter inside.

He'd been in the desk drawers, too, mine and Eberhardt's

both. And in my lockbox—the catch had been forced—but he hadn't taken any of the papers or petty cash. And in the file cabinets; the drawer marked G-K had been pawed through. Getting a little careless by that time, goddamn him, because he hadn't found what he'd come looking for. I hadn't had time to make up a file on the Grady Haas investigation, nor had I done a written report for Arlo Haas; and I had deposited his retainer check yesterday. When he'd called on Monday I had written his address and phone number in my pocket notebook. And he hadn't called since, while I was out, and left a message on the machine; I ran the tape just to make sure.

Oh, Blackwell had been thwarted, all right—but he wouldn't stay that way for long. What would his next move be? Would he come after me in person? Not openly or in the daylight hours, he wouldn't—not if I was reading him correctly. It seemed important to him to find Grady on the sly, to keep himself from being seen by potential witnesses. The way he'd handled Todd Bellin proved that; so did his break-in here. And he didn't know that I already had a description of him. Figure him for a police record; he might even be wanted somewhere. That would explain all the names he used too.

I sat at my desk. The anger in me was combustible; I slammed my fist down on the blotter. I'd let myself believe he didn't know about me, didn't know I was hunting him. Well, he knew, all right; he'd known for a couple of days now.

Savarese had told him.

Savarese and Blackwell, thick as thieves, and Grady Haas —and now me—smack in the middle.

IT WAS COLD along the bay, with a big wind that blew in over the ruined piers and sent litter swirling along China Basin Street. Gray sky, gray water, gray scavenger gulls filling the morning with their hungry shrieks. Tuesday's sun had given Savarese Importing's crumbling warehouse a touch of warmth and nostalgia, as with a historical relic that has fallen into disrepair; today, under the low gray ceiling, it had no charm at all. It was just a rotting hulk that stank of salt-decay and birdlime. Looking at it as I parked in front of the black iron fence, I wondered how it had survived the October quake relatively unscathed, while some of the structures nearby had suffered serious damage.

I had my anger in check now. But as I started across to the warehouse I warned myself to go slow and easy. I was more likely to open up Savarese with guile than with hard-ass threats and bluster.

Inside, the same skeleton crew was working in the same lethargic fashion. None of them even glanced at me as I climbed the creaky stairs to the second floor. The thin birdlike woman, Mabel, was hunched over her desk with her beak aimed downward into some kind of ledger. The other desk was empty. Mabel finally decided to acknowledge my presence, but only after I'd walked over close to her desk; and when she looked up at me it was the way a bird looks at you, sideways, because they can't see you straight on.

"Yes?"

"Mr. Savarese," I said.

"He's not here."

"I can see that. Is he in the building?"

"No."

"When do you expect him?"

"This afternoon. He's working at home this morning."

"Where would home be?"

"I can't tell you that."

"It's important, Mabel—"

"Mrs. Butler, if you don't mind."

"Sorry. It's important, Mrs. Butler."

"Be that as it may," she said. "You'll have to come back this afternoon."

"What time this afternoon?"

"After one o'clock. Is there a message?"

"No message."

She made a darting movement with her head, like a sparrow after a worm, and pointed her beak at the ledger again. I turned for the door, stopped, swung around to her again—one of those sly little afterthought maneuvers that Columbo always used to catch people off guard.

"Has Mr. Blackwell been in recently?" I asked her.

Up came up the head. "Who?"

"Mr. Blackwell."

"I don't know anyone named Blackwell."

"No? How about Jack King?"

"I don't know that name either."

"David Jones?"

". . . Are you playing some sort of game?"

"Not hardly," I said. "The man I'm interested in was here on April Fools' Day. Same day the woman from Intercoastal Insurance, Grady Haas, was here about the damaged-shipment claim."

Sparrow-eyed look: bright, shiny, blank.

"Mid-thirties," I said, "heavyset, short brown hair, nice tan, small curved scar under his right eye."

No reaction. Just "No," and the same blank look.

To hell with Columbo and his tricks. Life never imitates art when you want it to, anyway.

ON THE WAY ACROSS TOWN I used my mobile phone to call Harry Fletcher at the DMV and ask him to run Vernon Savarese's name, get me a home address. Harry bitched a little —his supervisors were riding herd, he said, ever since the new law prohibiting public access to private information about licensed drivers; and why didn't I quit calling him so damn often, if he lost his job it would be on *my* head. Harry's that way: a day without bitching is like a day without sunshine. The new law didn't have much to do with our working arrangement and he knew it as well as I did; it had been instituted to keep crazies from getting their claws on the home addresses and telephone numbers of celebrities. So I let him grumble, said some things to placate him, said I'd be at the office when he had the information, and rang off before he could start whining again.

When I got back to O'Farrell Street I found a locksmith working on the front door to my building, and the landlord, Sam Crawford—Sleazy Sam to those of us who didn't like him —throwing a minor tantrum in the presence of Martin Quon. Crawford wouldn't have cared if burglars had cleaned out everything belonging to his three tenants; he was upset because the door lock had been damaged and he had to pay for the installation of a new one.

He came after me as soon as I walked in. I hadn't told Martin that my office was the target of the break-in; nobody needed to know that but me. Let it look like an abortive B & E. But Crawford was cunning as well as penurious. He said, "This got something to do with you, don't it?" and poked me in the chest with his fat forefinger.

He had bad breath, body odor, and an outthrust belly that seemed to be trying to mate with mine. I said, "Poke me again and you'll be picking your fat up off the floor with both hands."

"What?" he said. "What? You can't talk to me like that—"

"Then keep your paws off me."

"I didn't hardly touch you. What's the idea?"

"I'm having a bad day and you're making it worse."

"Yeah? How'd you like your lease busted?"

"I wouldn't like it, Sam. Neither would you."

"That some kinda threat?"

"No more than the one you just made."

I shoved past him and into the elevator. The office was still shut up tight. No Eberhardt, and nothing from him on the answering machine. I would have been astonished if he'd been there or called.

I banged myself into my chair, caught up the phone—and froze with the receiver halfway to my ear as a paranoid thought worked its way through my head. Or maybe it wasn't paranoid; what did I know, really, about Blackwell? I unscrewed the mouthpiece, looked inside. Opened up the base unit and checked in there. No bug. Okay, so it *had* been a paranoid thought. The hell with it.

First call: Arlo Haas. Everything was status quo there. He'd just spoken to Constanza Vargas, he said. No change in Grady's attitude. I didn't tell him about the break-in last night; there wasn't any sense in adding to his load of worry. But I did mention the connection between Blackwell and Vernon Savarese, and promised to let him know as soon as I had an idea of its nature.

Second call: Jack Logan at the Hall of Justice. He took down the Blackwell, King, and Jones names and the man's description and agreed to run a check through the National Crime Information Center in Washington. He also agreed to run Savarese's name through the Criminal Justice Information System, California's computer link-up operated by the state attorney general's office. Then he said, "Eb's fiancée called Wednesday, said the wedding's been cancelled, but she wouldn't give me any details. What's up?" I told him what was up. He said, "Think it might help if I talked to Eb like a Dutch uncle?" I said it might but I knew it wouldn't.

Calls three through fourteen: Another canvass of the rental-car agencies on the dark brown Buick. This time around I provided the Blackwell name, but it got me no more than the King or Jones names had. If he'd rented the car locally, he'd used still another name. And it wouldn't have been his own either.

Fifteenth call: Eberhardt's home. I didn't expect an answer and I didn't get one; he hadn't even bothered to put his answering machine on today.

Sixteenth call: Kerry at Bates and Carpenter. The sound of her voice was enough to cheer me a little. I asked her if she'd like to have lunch. She'd like it, she said, but she couldn't; she was breaking bread with a client at one o'clock.

"How about tonight, then?" I asked. "Can you get away?"

"If Cybil's in good spirits. She was this morning."

"Good. I need a friendly ear."

"Among other friendly parts of my anatomy, hmm?"

"Always. But the friendly ear most of all."

"What's the matter? You sound down."

"Lousy day. And it's not even half over."

"Eberhardt?"

"He's one of the reasons. I went out to see him yesterday afternoon and we had a fight."

"So what else is new."

"No, I mean literally. I knocked him down."

"Oh, God. You didn't hurt him?"

"Just some more of his pride. But I feel guilty as hell about it."

"Have you talked to him since?"

"No. He didn't come in again today, naturally. I tried calling him a few minutes ago, but if he's home he's not answering the phone."

"So what are you going to do?"

"I don't know. That's why we need to talk. Maybe between us we can come up with an idea that'll get him and Bobbie Jean back together. And some way to patch things up between him and me."

We settled on seven o'clock at my flat. Unless there were problems with Cybil, and then Kerry would call and let me know.

I considered calling Bobbie Jean at work—she was a secretary to a real-estate broker in San Rafael—but I still couldn't seem to nerve myself up to it. What was I going to say to her? I was trying to think of something when the phone bell went off.

Harry Fletcher at the DMV. "You owe me big this time," he said. "Super caught me and I had to lie like a congressman to save my ass."

"I feel for you, Harry. How about if I throw in an extra five bucks per cheek?"

"Funny," he said. "But I'll hold you to the extra ten."

"You haven't earned it yet. Savarese's home address?"

"Eighty-two hundred Gellert Drive."

"Here in the city?"

"Here in the city."

"What kind of car does he drive?"

"You didn't ask me to find that out."

"Come on, Harry. You know me and I know you—I didn't ask, but you checked it anyway. What kind of car?"

"Plymouth Voyager. 'Eighty-eight."

"License number?"

He gave it to me.

"You're a prince, Harry. Don't let that super do anything to your ass."

He said cleverly, "Screw you, pal," and hung up on me.

Chapter 15

I HAD TO LOOK UP Gellert Drive on my city map. It was out on the western rim, in the Parkside District—close to Lake Merced and not far from the zoo. One of San Francisco's older middle-class residential neighborhoods, not quite as affluent an address as I'd expected for the owner of a fairly large import-export company.

I drove out there, and the house wasn't much even by neighborhood standards. It was on the part of Gellert that curves around to parallel Sunset: small, boxy, made of cinnamon-colored stucco with a brick facade, fronting on a narrow parkstrip that separated Gellert from Sunset's four-lane expanse. The garage was attached—door closed, no car in the driveway or parked in front—and on top of it was what looked to be a sundeck, wood-railed and lined along the front edge with potted palms.

Nobody answered the doorbell. Soft scraping sounds—not from inside but from somewhere overhead—kept me from pushing it again. The sundeck? I turned off the porch, and when I looked up a plumpish blond woman with a bright green scarf tied around her head was leaning against the rail between two of the potted palms, staring down at me.

"You want something?" she said.

No, I thought irritably, I'm just going around the neighborhood ringing doorbells; it's not much of a hobby but it keeps me from mugging old ladies. I said, "Vernon Savarese. Is he home?"

"No."

"Went down to China Basin, did he?"

"He didn't say where he was going."

I said, "Can you tell me—" but she wasn't there anymore.

I hesitated, listening to her move around up there. Then I walked over to the far side of the garage and along a narrow strip of lawn to the rear. A set of stairs, built onto the back of the garage, led up to the sundeck. I climbed them, calling out that I was coming so I wouldn't startle her.

Green AstroTurf on the sundeck, some rusty outdoor furniture, and the blonde standing there watching me with hostile eyes, one hand on her hip and the other clutching a plastic watering can as if she were getting ready to throw it at me. It was colder up there than down below. Even though the cloud cover was breaking up and there was sunlight on the deck, the wind blowing straight in off the ocean had a salty bite to it. It was rough in her hair and playful under the scarf, billowing and flapping the green cloth.

"What's the idea?" she said. "You think he's hiding up here? I told you, he went off somewhere."

"I just wanted to ask you a couple more questions," I said through a reassuring smile. "I didn't want to shout them for the neighbors to hear."

She made a derisive sound. "Fuck the neighbors."

What do you say to that?

"So what are you," she said, "a bill collector?"

"No. I've got other business with Mr. Savarese."

"I'll bet. Another damn bill collector."

"May I ask who you are?"

"Why?"

"I understood he was divorced. You wouldn't be his wife?"

"Me? Hell no. I'm his bimbo."

"His what?"

"His bimbo," she said and laughed, but not as if she thought anything was funny. "I'm the reason he got divorced."

"Oh."

"Yeah," she said. "His wife called me a bimbo, her lawyer called me a bimbo, the neighbors call me a bimbo, so I guess that's what I am, right?"

"Not necessarily."

She had a wide mouth, painted now with fuchsia lipstick, and she worked it into a self-mocking pout. The wind had loosened her scarf; she pulled it back into place, managed to retie it under her chin without letting go of the watering can. She was in her early thirties, attractive in a crusty, hard-edged sort of way, like a sugar cookie baked too long and then allowed to go stale. "So what is it you want, if you're not a bill collector?"

"I told you, I have some business with Mr. Savarese. It has to do with Mr. Blackwell."

"Who?"

"Blackwell." I described him. "You know the man?"

"No. Why should I?"

"I thought maybe he'd been out here to see Mr. Savarese."

"Well, he hasn't been. Not while I was here anyway. Vern doesn't do business at home if he can help it. Not that he does much business anywhere, these days."

"Things slow, are they?"

"You ought to know."

"My business with him has nothing to do with the import-export trade."

"No? What does it have to do with?"

"That's between Mr. Savarese and me."

"I don't give a shit one way or another," she said. "Unless you got some money for him. You don't, I suppose?"

"No," I said.

"Good-bye," she said, and showed me her back and walked over to one of the potted palms.

I called to her, "One more question before I go. What time did he leave this morning?"

She started to water the palm, stopped, and kicked the pot instead. "Why the hell do I bother?" she said to herself. "Stick with me, baby, he says, you'll live in a mansion. Yeah. A rented mansion in the fogbelt, watering somebody else's fucking palm trees."

I asked the question again: "What time did he leave this morning?"

"Half an hour ago," she said without looking at me. "When you track lover boy down, tell him something for me, huh?"

"What's that?"

"Tell him Gloria said stick it in his ear."

SAVARESE WASN'T at his warehouse.

The sparrow woman, Mabel Butler, was not pleased to see me again so soon. No, she said through pursed lips, he hadn't come in yet. No, he hadn't called. No, she certainly didn't know where he was—and her tone added that she wouldn't tell me if she did.

I went back outside and sat in my car. It was one-fifteen by my watch. I kept on sitting there, waiting—half an hour, forty-five minutes. No sign of Savarese.

Hunger and restlessness finally prodded me into movement. But I didn't go far, just down to a café on Third Street. At two-thirty, full of a crabmeat sandwich and a glass of something that had been false-advertised as iced tea, I drove back to Savarese Importing. No Plymouth Voyager van among the cars parked inside and outside the front fence. I took myself upstairs again anyway, spoiled some more of Mabel Butler's afternoon and some more of mine: same questions, same answers. As Yogi Berra once said, it was just like déjà vu all over again.

BACK TO MY OFFICE, because I had no place else to go. And ten minutes after I arrived, I had a visitor: Bobbie Jean Addison.

"I hope you don't mind me just dropping in like this," she said. "I know you're busy. . . ."

"No, no, I'm glad you came."

Wan smile.

"Sit down," I said. "How about some coffee?"

She accepted the first invitation, declined the second. She was wearing an electric blue pantsuit, and a little blue cap, and more makeup than she usually applied—an effort, I thought, to present a bright and cheerful facade. But there wasn't much cheer in her lean, angular face, or in the dark smudges under her eyes that powder and paint couldn't quite conceal. Normally Bobbie Jean is an attractive, animated woman who looks five years younger than fifty-one. Today, in spite of the window dressing, she looked five years older. Even her voice, usually husky, with traces of a drawl that betrays her South Carolina origins, had a flat intonation.

"I drove in to see Eb," she said. "I thought . . . well, that I could get him to talk things out. It's been three days now; one of us has to take the initiative."

"But you didn't see him?"

"No. He wasn't home."

"Not working either. Not for the past few days."

"I didn't expect to find him here. I came to see you."

"Oh?"

"I called Kerry a little while ago," Bobbie Jean said. "She told me about the fight yesterday."

Bobbie Jean and I have always been at ease in each other's company, but not today—at least not in my case. I felt acutely uncomfortable, and when I feel that way my hands turn into great twitching lumps of flesh. I put them in my lap, out of sight under the desk.

I said awkwardly, "I wanted to tell you about it myself. I started to call you last night and again this morning, but . . . well . . ."

"I know, you don't have to explain."

"I wanted to call Tuesday night too. But I'm just not good with words at times like that."

The wan smile again.

"I'm on your side in this, Bobbie Jean. One hundred percent. I want you to know that."

"I know it," she said. "It's why you had the fight with Eb, isn't it?"

I nodded. "Stupid, a stupid thing. Me hitting him, I mean. I shouldn't have done it—it only made things worse."

"He'll get over it."

"Sure," I said. "Sure he will."

Bobbie Jean was silent for a time. Then she said, "He's still angry at me, I suppose. Angry and bitter."

"Yes. I tried to talk some sense to him, get him to accept responsibility, but he wouldn't listen."

"Was he drinking?"

"Not then. But he had been—a two-day toot."

"You think he still is?"

"Last night, probably."

"He won't . . . I mean, you don't think he'll . . ."

"No, no way. A three-day bender is about his limit. Then he gets sick as a dog and can't stand even the smell of the stuff. That's how it was after his divorce and a couple of other times I know about."

"Well, at least I don't have to worry about *that.*"

"After he sobers up he'll listen to reason. Not from me, maybe, not after yesterday, but from you."

"I hope so," Bobbie Jean said. She ran her hands together in her lap, a dry raspy sound. "I keep telling myself I did the right thing, calling off the wedding, but I don't know . . .

he's so angry and hurt . . . I didn't think he'd take it this badly."

"It's his pride. He's got too much stubborn pride."

A nod, a sigh. "I should never have said yes in the first place. But he was so insistent, he kept after me and after me. . . ."

"He loves you."

"And I love him. Truly. Just not enough, I guess."

"Why do you say that?"

"If I loved him enough, I'd have gone through with the wedding no matter what. I *tried* to go through with it, God knows, but I just couldn't."

"That doesn't mean you don't love him enough."

"Maybe not. I had this feeling—I still have it—that if we got married the way he wanted us to, with all the pomp and circumstance, it wouldn't last. I've had two failed marriages, you know that, and I don't believe I could stand to go through another divorce. Not from Eb. Especially not from Eb."

"Did you tell him that?"

"Yes. He said I was being foolish."

"I don't think you're being foolish."

"But I shouldn't have waited so long," she said. "I should have put my foot down when he first started changing plans."

"What's that old saw? Hindsight's a great teacher?"

"Isn't it, though."

"You'll work it out, Bobbie Jean. You and Eb together."

"You really think he'll still want to?"

"Even if he won't admit it yet. I've known him thirty-odd years; sometimes I think I know him better than he knows himself."

"Then you can't believe, down deep, that what happened yesterday will damage your friendship. *I* know him well enough to know that he cares about you as much as you care about him."

"You and I are both right, then. I'll be an optimist if you will. Deal?"

"Deal," she said.

We talked a little longer, and when she left we hugged each other and I kissed her on the cheek. It had been a good few minutes for both of us. She'd come for reassurance, and given me some of the same in return. And maybe that's all any of us need to help us through the difficult times. A little reassurance. A little compassion and understanding. A little love.

AT FOUR-THIRTY I closed the office and made my third trip of the day to China Basin. The net result of which was another dose of frustration.

There was still no sign of Savarese's Plymouth Voyager van. I would have gone inside anyway, but it was just five o'clock and the warehouse crew was leaving for the day. I buttonholed the middle-aged philosopher I'd spoken to on Tuesday. No, he said, he hadn't seen the boss today. Didn't have no idea where he was or what he'd been doing instead of working. I described Blackwell for him and he allowed as how he might have seen somebody looked like that with the boss once; but he didn't know who the guy was or what his business might be.

"One thing he ain't," the philosopher said, "is a customer wants to buy the party crap we got in there. You can count on that, man, same as you can count on the freakin' government gouging us for more freakin' taxes."

Yeah. Freakin' right you could.

Chapter **16**

AS USUAL IN THE CITY, the Friday night rush-hour traffic was a bitch. It took me forty minutes to get from China Basin to Noe Valley, and I used back streets all the way. Bobbie Jean's visit had made me as determined to talk things out with Eberhardt as I was to track down Savarese and Blackwell; somebody had to start the machinery of apology that would lead to reconciliation, and it might as well be me.

But not tonight: Eb's car was gone and the house was dark. I would have taken a look inside, just the same, except that his spare key was no longer under the lava rock. I was not surprised.

I drove down to Twenty-fourth Street and poked my snout into the Shamrock Bar. He wasn't there either. Nor had he been in today; the bartender knew him. Some other watering hole in the neighborhood, maybe, but I had neither the time nor the patience to go bar-hopping. Eberhardt would just have to wait until tomorrow.

Gellert Drive was another washout. Savarese's driveway was empty and so was his garage; I looked through a side window to make sure. Nobody answered the door, not even Gloria, the self-styled bimbo.

The whole day now—no Savarese. Why? Where the hell was he?

I cut through the park and out Twenty-fifth Avenue to Clement. It was six-forty by then and I was hungry and there was a Thai-Chinese restaurant that did some fine things with a seafood mixture served in potato baskets. Rather than eating there I ordered takeout, two portions. Kerry might have to eat with Cybil first before she could get away; then again, she might not. Either way, the second order would not go to waste.

By the time I reached Pacific Heights, the food smell was making me drool on myself. But because it was Friday night and seven-thirty, there was no street parking on my block; I had to drive around for ten minutes before I found somebody pulling out of a space on Buchanan. The driving around tried what was left of my patience, and not just because I was hungry. One of the parked cars I passed was Kerry's.

I made short work of the three-block walk to my building. A crescendo of woodwinds and crashing cymbals greeted me —Dennis Litchak, the retired fire captain who lived downstairs, was a classical music buff—and the percussion followed me upstairs. Give me jazz any day: I've got short hair to go with my blue collar. I was thinking about that, and about Kerry, and about seafood in potato baskets, as I keyed open my door.

No lights. Just rooms full of clotted dark.

The wrongness of it was an immediate impact on my mind, as jarring as a physical blow. One second I was standing there looking in at the darkness; the next I was out of the doorway, up against the hallway wall beside it, muscles and nerves pinching tight all through my body.

Nothing happened.

Silence inside, so complete it was like a pressure against my eardrums. I stayed where I was, unmoving, for long dragging seconds. Still nothing—no sounds, not even the ghost of a noise. But the aura of wrongness remained; I could almost smell it, like a faint whiff of ozone before or after a storm.

Caution might have kept me where I was a while longer, except that my mind was full of Kerry now. I shoved off the wall, went in fast and low, going after the light switch with one up-sweeping hand. The ceiling globe and couchside lamp destroyed the dark but not the tension, not even when I saw that the living room was empty.

The room looked the same as always . . . no, not quite. One of the chairs was out of position, drawers in the secretary desk had been yanked open. I straightened, breathing hard, and took half a dozen strides, and then stopped again when I could see past the end of the couch, over in front of the fireplace.

Kerry's purse was lying on the hearth. On its side. Open.

A blood-surge of fear and rage drove me forward again, into the bedroom. She wasn't in there. Bathroom. No. Kitchen. No. Back porch. No, but the locks were off the door. I threw it open, stepped out onto the landing at the top of the alley stairs. Nothing to see below. I ran down into the alley anyway. Nobody there, just shadows and garbage smells and somebody's prowling cat.

Gone? On her own, got away from him? Or did he . . . ?

I pounded back upstairs, half-crazy now with fear, and tore through the flat again. And this time, almost immediately, I found her. Where I hadn't thought to look in those first frantic minutes.

In the bedroom closet. Lying crumpled on the floor of the bedroom closet.

I made some kind of noise as I went to my knees beside her and saw the blood on her face; made another kind of noise when I found that she was breathing and her pulse was strong, steady. I lifted her, gently, gently, and got her out of that narrow space and carried her to the bed. She moaned; one of her hands lifted, fell back across her chest. But she didn't open

her eyes. In the light from the bedside lamp I had a better look
at her face. Inch-long cut on her right cheekbone, not too
deep; bruise and weal on her left temple. He'd hit her with his
hands or some kind of weapon, beat her the same way he'd
beaten Todd Bellin, and then stuffed her in the goddamn
closet.

I'll kill him, I thought. I'll tear his heart out.

I bulled into the bathroom, fumbled the cold water faucet
on full stream. My hands were shaking; I dropped the wash-
cloth on the floor before I got it into the basin. Thoughts
stumbled against one another in my head: My fault. After
Bellin, after last night at the office . . . why didn't I figure he
might come here next? Why did I let *her* come here tonight,
alone? My fault she's hurt. Why wasn't I more careful?

I squeezed water out of the cloth, took it into the bedroom.
Kerry was still lying there with her eyes shut, twitching a little
now, rolling her head. I knelt beside her, held her still with my
left hand, sponged blood off the cut. She moaned again—and
her eyes popped open, blind in that first instant, shiny with
terror. She felt my hands on her, fought against them wildly,
crying out. I kept saying, "Kerry, it's me, it's all right, it's
me," until the words got through to her and her eyes focused
on my face. Then, all at once, she went limp. I held her, whis-
pering her name. For a time she clung to me, then pushed me
away. Reluctantly I let her go, drew back on my knees so I
could look into her face.

"I thought you were him," she said thickly.

"No, no."

"Did you . . . ?"

"No, he was gone before I got here. Don't talk for a minute."

I cleansed away the rest of the blood from her cheek. She
winced at the pressure on the cut, and I winced with her; it
was as if I could feel the pain myself.

She said, "God, I must be a mess."

"Not too bad. How do you feel?"

"Shaky. And my head hurts."

"Anywhere else? He hit you in the body?"

"No. Just . . . no."

"All right. Lie still for a while."

"Yes, doctor."

Weak joke, but the shadows of terror were still in her eyes. Inside me, the rage kept seething. I tried to show her a poker face, but I was afraid she could see some of what lay black and ugly behind it, that it would frighten her even more. *Turn your head* . . . but I could not make myself stop looking at her.

"Don't you want to know what happened?"

"When you're ready."

She pushed herself higher on the bed, reaching up for one of the pillows. I helped get it behind her head. When she was motionless again she said, "Get me some aspirin, okay? Then I'll tell you."

I went and got the aspirin and a glass of water. Before I came back out I looked at myself in the medicine cabinet mirror. The poker face was on tighter than I'd thought; you couldn't see any of the violence roiling inside like floodwaters against a dam.

"Ready?" I asked her when she'd swallowed the aspirin.

"Ready."

"Take your time. Go slow."

"I got here about six forty-five," she said. "Cybil wasn't hungry so I thought I'd come early, see if you were here and if you wanted to go somewhere for dinner. I didn't notice anybody on the street . . . I don't know where he was hiding. In one of the parked cars, or in the alley—"

"Wait a minute. He grabbed you outside?"

"In the vestibule, while I was unlocking the downstairs door."

"Crept up and caught you from behind?"

"Yes. He knew me, knew my first name . . . I don't know how."

I did: the photo of her on my office desk. She had signed it, on the front in ink: "With All My Love, Kerry." He hadn't been after her tonight; he had no way of knowing she was coming to see me. He'd been after me. But he'd recognized her when she came along the sidewalk, and she was an easier way into the flat than I would have been.

"What did he say to you?"

" 'Don't scream'. . . . He wouldn't hurt me as long as I was quiet. He had a gun, he poked me in the back with it." A little shiver went through her; goose bumps came up on her arms. "At first I thought . . . you know, rape. It's the first thing a woman thinks of in that situation."

"Then?"

"He told me to finish unlocking the door, go inside and climb the stairs. He seemed to know where your flat was."

"What else did he say?"

"Keep my eyes front. Don't try to turn my head and look at him or he'd make me sorry."

"You obeyed him?"

"You bet. He . . . I knew he meant it."

"What happened after you let him in here?"

"He told me to turn on the lights, keep looking straight ahead. Then he made me stop; I guess he was looking around. Then he took my purse . . . I don't know what he did with it. . . ."

"It's in the front room."

"Well, he didn't look inside it then. He told me to walk in here. I thought . . . I still had rape on my mind. But that wasn't what he was after. He let go of me and said to turn around slowly. That was when . . . the first time he hit me. I yelled, or started to—I *think* I yelled—and that's all I remember." She winced again, touched the bruise on her temple. "He must have hit me more than once, damn him."

"You see him at all, even a glimpse?"

"No. Just . . . he was a shape, that's all."

"All right," I said.

"You know who he is, though, don't you? What he was after?"

"Yeah. I know who he is and what he was after."

"The Grady Haas case?"

"Yes." I'd been kneeling beside the bed; now I got to my feet. "Rest, babe. I want to look around some more."

I turned before she could say anything else, walked out quick into the living room. There was a squeezed-up sensation in my chest; I was having trouble breathing. In the kitchen I ran cold water into the sink and doused my head. It helped a little. I made myself take air in slow, shallow inhalations and that helped too.

Living room again. Kerry's purse. He'd rifled it but it didn't look as though he'd taken anything. Why should he? He wasn't a sneak thief any more than he was a rapist. He'd been through the desk . . . every drawer and cubbyhole in the place, probably. But it hadn't done him a lick of good. I still carried the notebook with Arlo Haas's name and address, and there was nothing else here—

Answering machine, I thought.

Into the bedroom. The message light was off; but if it had been on and he'd listened in, he might have rewound the tape again afterward. Kerry lay quiet, watching me, as I pushed the *play* button and stood listening. Harvey, the bell captain at the Broadmoor Hotel, saying that he had some things to tell me . . . old message, from last night. None since then; none from Arlo Haas. Nothing for Blackwell on the answering machine either.

Then why hadn't he waited for me to come home? He'd come here after *me,* to pump *me,* and yet he'd left after or at some point during his search. Why, if he hadn't found a lead to Grady's whereabouts?

I didn't see how he could have. And yet I couldn't see any other reason for him to have quit the flat—and in something of a hurry, too, through the back door. I didn't like it. It added even more urgency to the hatred inside me.

I said to Kerry, "How do you feel? Well enough to be up and around?"

"I think so."

"I've got to go out and I don't want to leave you here alone. I'll drive you home—"

"No," she said. "I can drive myself."

"I don't think that's a good idea."

"I don't think it's a good idea for you to go after him, either, but you're going to and I won't try to stop you. Do what you have to do. Let me do what I have to do."

"If you're sure . . ."

"I'm sure. Go on, go. Don't wait for me. I want to wash my face, make myself look presentable, so I don't give Cybil a coronary when I get home. I'll be all right; he's not going to come back here tonight."

"Kerry . . ."

"I know," she said. "I love you too. Just take care of yourself, okay? And don't do anything . . . crazy because of what happened to me. Promise me that."

"I promise," I said, and I wasn't sure if I was lying or not.

I kissed her, touched her cheek, went away from her.

The front door, I saw as I started for it, was shut. I must have closed it at some point, but I couldn't remember doing that. I opened it, and lying on the carpet in the hallway were the Thai-Chinese take-out dinners, one of the cartons split and leaking seafood sauce. I also had no memory of dropping the cartons.

The smell of the food, once so appetizing, now made my gorge rise. I bent and picked up the containers and carried them into the kitchen and dumped them in the garbage. I don't know why I took the time to do that, unless it was because at some level I did not want Kerry to have to deal with any more of my messes.

Chapter 17

THE SAVARESE HOUSE was still dark, apparently still empty. I went up to the door anyway, rang the bell, shook the thing by the knob and kicked it a couple of times, foolishly. Nothing. The idea was in my head to break and enter, search the place, but that was foolish, too, and I didn't give in to it.

When I came back toward my car I noticed that the garage door was raised at the neighboring house on the north and that there was a light on inside. I detoured over that way, walked up the drive. The garage was packed floor-to-ceiling with cartons, furniture, gardening equipment, hundreds of other items; you couldn't have fit a go-cart inside there, let alone an automobile. At first I didn't see anybody among the maze of stuff, but I could hear random noises. I moved closer, calling out, and pretty soon a little guy about seventy poked his head around a stack of boxes and gave me a squinty look.

"I'm looking for Vernon Savarese," I said. "You happen to have seen him tonight?"

"Nope."

"So you wouldn't have any idea where I can find him?"

"Nope."

"How about his lady friend, Gloria?"

"Lady friend," the old guy said and laughed. "If she's a lady, I'm the Duke of Windsor."

"I really need to talk to Savarese," I said. "Any help you can give me . . ."

"Sorry, bub. I don't know where they are and I don't much care. I just hope it's far away and they don't come back too soon."

"Why is that?"

"Lousy neighbors, that's why," he said. "Fight all the time, day and night. And the language . . . you never heard such foul language. Her especially. Woman's got a mouth that would shame the devil himself."

"What do they fight about?"

"Money, mostly. You're not a friend of theirs, eh?"

"No."

"Bill collector?"

"You might say that. I'm trying to collect a debt."

"Don't surprise me," he said. "Deadbeats, that's what those two are. I happen to know they're two months behind in their rent and the landlord's threatened to evict 'em. Be the best thing for the neighborhood if that happens."

"You know any of their friends? Anybody I can contact who might know where Savarese is?"

"Nope. I mind my own business, even if they don't mind theirs."

I nodded to him, turned back down the drive.

"Good luck, mister. I sure hope you collect that debt."

"I will," I said. "Sooner or later, one way or another."

I DIDN'T EXPECT to find Savarese at his China Basin warehouse, but I drove down there anyway because I had no-where else to look for him. And a light was on inside the building, a wedge of it coming through a man-sized gap be-tween the entrance doors. And parked in front of the fence, sitting there all by itself, was a light-colored van—a Plymouth Voyager.

In my mind again I saw Kerry lying crumpled in the bedroom closet, the blood on her face, the bruise on her temple. I could feel heat rising, the sudden pound of blood in my ears; the palms of my hands were moist. I had to force myself not to whip the car in behind the van, go rushing into the warehouse. Instead I drove on past, down toward Mission Rock, checking the few other cars parked in the area. Ratty clunkers, most of them, temporary homes for the homeless. I turned around, came back past Savarese Importing in the opposite direction. No dark brown Buick anywhere in the vicinity.

All right. Just Savarese, then. In there alone, working tonight because he hadn't worked during the day. All right. Him first, get some answers, and then that other son of a bitch.

I parked near the deserted private boat club, went the rest of the way on foot—walking fast but not running. Dark night, cold, the wind needle-sharp against my face. Foghorns on the bay, their voices rising and falling in monotonous warning even though the mist here was high and thin, drifting like smoke under the higher overcast. Lights from the Bay Bridge and from the shipyards put a dull-bright sheen on the darkness, made the water look thick and oily where it lapped in against the ruined piers. No cars, no pedestrians moved along China Basin Street; out here I had the night to myself.

The gate in the iron fence was closed but not locked. I eased it open, walked quiet across the empty parking area. Overhead lights were on in the front part of the warehouse, and when I stepped inside I could see that the windowed wall along the front part of the ell was also lighted. The back half of the building was inky with shadow.

I paused near the stairwell. The air in there was even chillier, moister, than outside. Random thought: Wouldn't the salt-damp damage stored paper goods after a while? Well, maybe Savarese couldn't afford to heat the place; that was probably it. Before I started up the stairs I listened. Silence. Out on the bay, faintly, the moaning voice of the foghorns. Silence. Scurrying noise somewhere in the back-half darkness: rat on the move. Silence.

I went up on the balls of my feet, to keep the stair risers from creaking and announcing my presence. As I approached the open door to the office I could see that the lights were on in there too. I stopped again, just outside. Didn't hear anything and went on in.

The room was empty.

What the hell? I thought. Then I thought: Maybe he's in the toilet. I started toward his desk at the far wall.

Sounds in the hallway behind me: door hinges creaking, soft shuffling footfalls.

I pulled up short, heeled around—and somebody was moving behind the fire door, arm and shoulder and hip visible at the edge, shoving the door inward fast and hard. I ran that way, heard the clang of metal as it banged shut a second or two before I slammed into it with my shoulder. I bounced off, pain running down my right side, and came back again and fumbled for the knob . . . key scraping in the lock . . . too late again.

Trap, goddamn trap.

And I had blundered right into it, as blindly and stupidly as if I'd been that rat downstairs.

I YANKED ON THE KNOB, twisted and pulled and shook the door, let go of it after a few seconds and beat on the metal with my fist. Quit that, breathing hard, and leaned against the door to listen. Faint sounds, but not in the hallway —somewhere down below. Then nothing. Savarese? Hadn't looked like him, what little I'd seen of the man behind the door. Blackwell, then. Alone? Or was Savarese here too?

Why?

Why lock me in here like this?

I swung around to face the office again. Telephone on Mabel Butler's desk. I went to it, caught up the receiver. No dial tone. The phone on Savarese's desk was just as dead. Did something to the wires so I couldn't call out. No window in here, no way in or out except the door. Perfect set-up for a snare . . . and it hadn't been arranged by Savarese. Blackwell's work. He knew I'd come looking for him as soon as I found Kerry; knew I had no way to find him except through Savarese; knew I'd show up here tonight sooner or later. Put the lights on, left the gate and front doors unlocked, disabled the phones, sat back and waited.

Why?

He knows where Grady is, I thought. Somehow he found out and he's going after her and he wants me out of commission for a couple of days, give himself plenty of time to find her, get rid of her, get away . . . no, hell, that doesn't add up. Leave me alive and I can tie him to her; he can't be sure of how much I might have found out about him. Why not just shoot me, dump me in the bay? But if he *doesn't* know where she is, why didn't he brace me the way he braced Kerry? Either way, it doesn't add up. . . .

Back at the door, I bent to look at the lock. Yale lock, one of the best; you'd need to be a locksmith to get it open and even then you'd have to have the proper tools. I ran my finger along the edge of the door where it met the jamb. Tight fit, with what was probably a quarter-inch metal overlap on the outside; that was standard on fire doors of this type. No way I was going to get through it until somebody came with a key.

I laid my ear against the cold metal. Still the same faint noises: somebody moving around, either downstairs or up here at the rear of the ell. The sounds were unidentifiable. Nor could I tell if they were being made by one man or two.

Rising tension set me to prowling the office. There was not much to it, just a big room thirty feet square, on the cluttered side, not too clean. Savarese's desk, Butler's desk, a third desk that looked as though it hadn't been used in a while, nothing on it except a cheap portable copy machine and a FAX machine. Utility table, piled high with product brochures and

samples of Taiwanese party supplies. Water bottle upended on
a pottery stand. Three-drawer metal filing cabinet. Door in the
inner wall, partially open so I could see into a cramped supply
closet. Nothing in the closet or anywhere else in the office that
I could use as a pry bar or battering ram, except maybe one of
the drawers in the filing cabinet; and trying to pound my way
through a metal door with a metal file drawer was like trying
to knock down a brick house with a single brick.

Back and forth, back and forth, with the tension and the
frustration climbing all the while. Rat in a closed-off maze,
hunting for a way out that wasn't there. Cold in here; I could
see my breath each time I exhaled. Cold, cramped, the air stale
with must and old tobacco smoke and salt-damp. How the hell
could they work in an office like this? No windows, no fresh
air, it would be like spending eight hours in a goddamn box—
Shrinking now . . . the box seemed to be shrinking
around me.

I could feel it start to happen, the sudden shift in perception, the claustrophobic closing in. Then the sweating, the
shaking. Dark things skittered in the corners of my mind, little
fear-shapes dragging forth scraps of memory.

*Interior of that rustic mountain cabin—cold, barren, blank
walls, window looking out on empty landscape, cot with its
stinking blankets, shelves and boxes and the little bathroom
cubicle . . . and the heavy iron shackle around my leg, the
attached chain slithering and clanking when I move . . . and
the fear . . . and the screaming loneliness . . . and the walls,
ceiling, floor all shrinking, squeezing me in. . . .*

For a few seconds I couldn't breathe. I stumbled to the
Butler woman's desk, leaned on it with my eyes shut tight and
my head down, fighting the terror, using all the clever little
mental defenses I'd concocted in the cabin and in the months
after my escape. A minute, two minutes, and the worst of it
was over. Wobbly-legged, I groped around the desk and sat
down in the chair that went with it. I was still hyperventilat-
ing; I willed myself to take air in slow, deep breaths until my

pulse rate slowed. Sweat flowed on me, kept flowing. But when I opened my eyes the walls were no longer contracting and the room was just a room and the images of the Deer Run cabin were buried again in their shallow graves.

I sat quiet, not letting myself think about anything, until my pores closed and the sweat dried on my body. Then, slowly, I got up and returned to the door. This time when I listened there was nothing to hear except the distant grieving of the foghorns.

Turn around, walk. Savarese's desk against the far wall: Would he leave anything incriminating in there? Find out— something to do with your hands and your mind.

Clutter. Every drawer full of a miscellany of papers, stationery supplies, odd items that ranged from cheap cigars to pieces of caramel candy to a well-thumbed deck of pornographic playing cards. I shuffled through the papers. Random business correspondence, dun notices for unpaid bills, business cards, scraps with writing in a crabbed hand I took to be Savarese's. Some of the scraps bore names, addresses, telephone numbers, but none of the names was Blackwell or King or Jones and none of the addresses was familiar.

No appointment calendar on his desk, but there was one on Mabel Butler's. I opened it, flipped back through the pages to April Fools' Day and then forward again a page at a time. Not many notations, and none that meant anything to me. I pawed through the drawers; nothing there either. Filing drawers next. Bills of lading, invoices paid and unpaid, business correspondence . . . nothing.

I slammed the last drawer shut, went back to Savarese's desk. A big green ink-stained blotter covered a good portion of its surface. I lifted it to see if there was anything underneath.

Dust and some more pieces of paper. I shuffled through the papers, stopped shuffling when I came to a pair of Visa card receipts. One bore the name of Panotti's North Beach restaurant, and the date on it was a week ago Tuesday—the night Savarese and Blackwell had had dinner together there.

The other receipt had been issued at the Harborside Inn and the date on that one was last Saturday. The Harborside was a Fisherman's Wharf hotel, on Beach Street—not in the same class as the Broadmoor, but similarly small and quiet and moderately expensive.

Was that where Blackwell had moved after leaving the Broadmoor? The amount on the receipt was eighteen dollars and change, the price of drinks for two people. The Harborside wasn't the kind of place Savarese was likely to take Gloria the bimbo; the bar there, as I recalled, didn't offer entertainment or much of a view and was mainly patronized by paying guests. Savarese and Blackwell again, with their heads together? Cooking up what?

Fisherman's Wharf was only a few miles from here, at the other end of the Embarcadero. If I could just get out of this trap . . .

Back to the door. This time I heard something: not the sounds of movement as before, but a vague murmuring. No, not a murmuring—a kind of crackling, as if somebody were balling up a sheet of cellophane. I kept listening. The crackling remained steady, distant, not gaining in volume. Smell in the air too, now, just as faint. Acrid smell, smoke smell—

Fire?

Jesus—*fire*?

I shoved back off the door. And the whole thing began to open up in my mind, hazy but complete, like a materializing ghost: the purpose of the trap, the relationship between Savarese and Blackwell, who and what Blackwell was and the reason he was after Grady Haas.

Part of my attention was on that, the rest on a desperate scan for some way out of here, when the explosion hurled everything into chaos.

Cracking, booming concussion, the floor shuddering, buckling under my feet . . . and I was thrown backward with things flying all around me . . . I hit something, went up in the air and over a hard surface and down in a crazy somersault

. . . eruption of pain in my head and neck, burst of light, fragments of color . . . and then a heaving darkness filled with a discordant medley of sounds that seemed to go on and on . . . until I went deaf.

Chapter **18**

I COULD NOT HAVE BEEN OUT, or partially out, for more than three or four minutes. Then the darkness shimmered, receded, and I could see all right—but at first I didn't know what I was seeing. Confusion, pain . . . and when that eased I was aware of lying twisted up on the floor with a heavy weight pinning my legs, and that there was smoke in the air. I could hear again, too, a far-off noise I knew was the crackle-thrum of fire.

I flailed around with my arms, maneuvered my lower body until I was able to free one leg and then the other. I had been thrown against the far wall and Savarese's chair and one corner of his desk were what had been pinning me. I got up on one knee, shoved the desk out of the way so I could stand.

The office looked the way mine had after the October earthquake, as though it had been shaken by angry hands: furniture knocked askew and overturned, the water bottle and its stand broken, papers strewn around like patches of dirty snow. Smoke-haze gave the upheaval a nightmarish cast. The explosion had buckled the floor in places . . . and sprung the lock on the metal door, by God, so that the door was now cracked open a couple of inches. That was how the smoke, blackish and virulent, was slithering in—not too thick yet but getting thicker.

I groped around Savarese's desk, across to the door. But when I threw my shoulder against it, the crack widened only another inch or so before the warped lower edge bound up and held fast. I hit it again, twice, but it was wedged tight against one of the buckled places in the hallway floor. Panic rose in me. A little wildly I kicked at the bottom of the door, straight on and then with the sole of my shoe. No use either way. I could not get enough leverage to drive it past the obstruction.

The congealing smoke was raw in my lungs, and my eyes were streaming tears. Coughing, working to clear my vision, I came away from the door. When I could see again I looked for the broken water bottle. The bottom hadn't completely shattered; the biggest of the heavy shards lay curved in such a way that it still cradled maybe a cupful of water. I soaked my handkerchief, cleansed my eyes, then tied the wet cloth, bandit-fashion, over my nose and mouth. That let me breathe a little easier.

The beat of the fire was louder, closer. I could feel the heat of it coming through the floor, making steam rise from the wetness under the remains of the water bottle. No flames to see yet—just the smoke curling in through the crack in the door.

Mabel Butler's desk was the smallest of the three in there and the closest to the door. Made of metal, with sturdy legs on casters. I got around behind it, maneuvered it into a direct line with the door. One of the casters had come off and it moved awkwardly, but there was no time to go hunting the thing. I threw all my weight against the desk, legs driving hard, and sent it rolling and wobbling and then clanging into the door. The impact jarred me, almost knocked me down. But the door didn't break free. Yielded another inch, maybe, that was all. The gap was still too narrow for me to squeeze through.

I dragged the desk backward, repositioned it. Even with the wet handkerchief, each breath was painful and I was coughing fitfully again. There was a chemical stench to the smoke that made my head pound, built nausea in the back of my throat. Dizzy, light-headed . . . *move!* I ran the desk forward again, metal hammering against metal, and the door held, and I dragged the desk back and ran it forward, and the door held, and gasping now I dragged the desk back and ran it forward—

And the door gave. Not much, not so that I could get it all the way open, but enough to widen the gap to more than a foot.

More smoke poured in, set me to gagging as I clawed the desk out of the way, squeezed my body into the opening. Then I was out into the hallway, bent double, blind in a cocoon of churning, stinking smoke. My stomach convulsed; vomit came boiling up out of me. The spasms were brief but they left me weak and clinging to the near wall.

I was aware then of the rising sound of sirens. Somebody must have heard the explosion or seen the fire right away and turned in the alarm. There was a fire station on the Embarcadero not far away, housing the 35 Engine company and the city's fireboat; and the S.F.F.D. has one of the best response times in the country. Men and equipment would be here any minute—

—but they'd find me dead if I didn't get off this ell. *Move, move!*

I got the wet handkerchief back in place, pulled myself along the wall with outstretched hands. The hallway floor was littered with broken glass; shards crunched each time I put my foot down. The windows had all burst inward from the force of the blast and the smoke was churning up through the openings from below. Here and there I could see flames where little jagged holes had been blown open in the floorboards. The heat was already intense.

All the long way from the office to the stairwell I managed to avoid the holes, keep from plunging through the weakened boards. But the stairs were no way out: fire was on them, eating upward from riser to riser, pulsing demonically in the hazed dark. Only a minute or two and the fire would be up here . . . if it hadn't already completed its climb at the rear of the ell.

I plowed past the stairwell, stumbling on the uneven floor, leaning against the wall again to maintain my balance. There didn't seem to be any tears in the boards down here, but the footing was still uncertain. Blind, groping movements brought me to the end of the wall, where the hallway opened up into the ell's short arm. Then I could see again because the smoke was thinner back there. The panic cut at me, sharp-edged. Flames were crawling up the dry-rotted far wall, running across the floor and just beginning to lick at stacks of boxes and drums.

No choice: I lumbered ahead to the left, away from the fire. Looking frantically for another way down.

The smoke was too dense, the firelight too weak, the storage area too crowded: I couldn't make out anything except hazy shapes. I tripped over something, staggered, righted myself. There was a dull shattering noise, the clink and splatter of falling glass—heat, or some fire-flung object, fragmenting one of the windows in the back wall. The incoming surge of wind fanned the flames, threw some of them my way; let in the banshee shriek of sirens. Through the opening I had a glimpse of the light-shimmer from Mission Rock Terminal. Then the dirty glass in one of the unbroken windows went bloodred— the pulsars on arriving fire trucks.

Get to the nearest window, break the glass, go out that way. But I didn't do it. Last resort. If I tried jumping without a net, the drop to the cement pier was enough to break bones, maybe break my head. And I couldn't just stand there yelling and waiting for the firemen to spot me and set up a net; there was no time, not the way that blaze was soaring now.

Another window burst; more inrushing wind, more noise from outside—shouts, the grind and throb of heavy equipment being maneuvered into place. The entire far wall was an in-

ferno. Flames ran along the girders under the roof, heating
them and the sheet metal above like iron in a forge. But now
the fire gave off enough glittering light for me to distinguish
most of what lay around me and at the back wall. No staircase, no freight elevator . . . but there *had* to be one or the
other; where the hell was it?

A tier of cardboard drums obscured part of the northeast
corner. I blundered around the drums, and then I could see it
—a freight elevator like a black-gated hole in the firelit wall.
When I got to the gate I had to lean against it for a few
seconds to battle air into my clogged lungs, to cleanse sweat
out of my eyes. The elevator was on this floor . . . a piece of
luck if the fire hadn't yet burned out the electrical system, a
funeral pyre for me if it had.

I heaved the gate up, stepped inside, threw the gate back
down. I couldn't see the controls clearly, had to fumble
around until I located the panel and the two buttons on it.
Nothing happened when I punched one of the buttons . . .
oh Christ . . . and I felt the hot breath of the flames and
jabbed frantically at the second button.

A whine, a whir, a sudden jerking motion, and the elevator
began to grind downward.

Relief jellied my legs; I leaned panting on the gate. The
handkerchief was all but dry from the heat and no longer
acting as much of a filter . . . pass out if I didn't get clear of
the smoke pretty quick and the elevator seemed to be creeping,
creeping. I couldn't see any of the lower floor—and then I
could, a hairline of it that slowly widened until I was looking
into a seething cauldron of smoke and flame. Steam, too, from
melted sprinkler heads and the first jets of water from firemen's hoses out front. Sparks erupted here, there, in a succes-
sion of bright blooms. The images were mad, surreal, like a
Cotton Mather vision of the Old Testament netherworld.

The elevator shuddered, suddenly stopped.

But it hadn't come all the way down; the floor was still a
couple of feet below me. I jabbed at the control button. Noth-

ing happened—the electrical system was gone. I yanked on the gate, couldn't get it to lift; crawled clumsily over the top of it; lost my grip before I was ready to let go. Short drop, but my feet went out from under me and I was down in a rushing convergence of blue-edged flames. The heat drove me right back up again. It felt as though the soles of my shoes were burning.

More glass splintered somewhere. Thirty yards away fire and ugly coils of black smoke vomited out of a jumble of bales and barrels. I threw an arm up over my head, lurched away from the elevator.

When I came out from under the ell, into the cleared area in the middle of the warehouse, I could see most of the way to the front, where the fire was hottest. Portions of the front wall were a mass of flame. Hammering noises came from the roof up that way: firemen on aerial ladders trying to cut ventilation holes. I took a couple of shambling strides toward the back wall—and then stopped when something else caught my eye through the swirls and billows.

Man-shape, loosely sprawled and smouldering, partway up the center aisle.

Despite the heat and the smoke-blockage in my lungs, I changed direction, took myself toward the blackened form. The stench of cooked flesh reached me before I reached him, made me gag and then vomit again dryly as I moved. He lay facedown, one leg drawn up toward his middle. Charred, roasted to a cinder: little tongues of fire still licked hungrily along his back and buttocks. Dead—long dead. I didn't need to see his face, if he had a face anymore, to recognize him. The size and shape of his corpse were enough.

Savarese.

Blackwell's deathtrap hadn't been just for me; it had been designed for Savarese too. Eliminate two threats at once. Cook two birds in one giant oven.

The heat drove me back, into a sharp about-face. Toward the rear, a dull muffled thunder came from the roof: extra-heavy streams of water pounding violently against the super-heated sheet metal. The whole building seemed to tremble under the impact. More sparks erupted; fragments of crate-lumber rocketed upward, then fell in blazing parabolas. One of the fragments landed on my left arm, burned fast through the cloth of my coat sleeve. I felt a jolt of pain, smelled again the stink of burning flesh before I could swipe the thing off.

The rear loading doors were visible ahead, shimmering in the fireglow; I stumbled toward them on legs of iron and splinters. Scalding water, streaming from the roof, ran down the back of my neck. There was a pulsing pressure in my eardrums, but faintly I could hear men yelling outside, the throbbing roar of some kind of big engine. I tried to shout as I ran, to let the firefighters know I was in here, but I had too little breath and a throat as dry as sand.

Sudden low booming, like a mortar shell going off. Almost instantly the air cleared and the constriction in my chest eased and the pressure in my ears was gone. Part of the front wall must have collapsed, or there had been an explosive backdraft through one of the ventilation holes—releasing pent-up gases, feeding fresh oxygen to the inferno. Around me the flames seemed to lift and soar. The heat against my back was a thrusting force.

Frizzling, crispy sound: my hair starting to singe. Jesus! Heat in here must be nearing 175 degrees. A few degrees more and the wax in my ears would melt, slosh around like water; and at a few degrees above that, my ears and nose would blister and then all of me would ignite like a struck match. . . .

I was thirty feet from the doors when the jet of water hit them full on, burst them apart with terrific force. One instant I was running, streaming sweat, close to collapsing from the heat, the next I was engulfed by icy brackish water, down on the floor, being rolled over and swept sideways. I banged into something, caught hold of something else and managed to hang on, gasping, choking . . . and then the stream quit punishing my body, lifted and aimed higher. The water that fell on me then was like a hard, steady rain.

I flopped over, got up on one knee, brushed at my eyes until I could see. The loading doors had been driven wide open and now the stream of water was lifting toward the roof. Underneath it, firemen were moving inside, the first wave of them crouched behind the wide-angle spray of a fog nozzle. The ones behind them carried powerful flashlights, wore plastic helmets and oxygen masks and Scott Air-Pak tanks on their backs: rescue squad.

I hauled my feet under me, stood, managed to stay upright. I still couldn't make any sounds but it didn't matter now. It only took a couple of seconds for one of the torches to find me.

"Over there!" I heard the squaddie shout. "Man alive over there!"

They ran and I ran and I would have fallen if hands hadn't caught and held me. An urgent voice against my ear asked if anybody else was in the building. I choked out a response: "One man but he's dead."

Deft fingers laid a Scott mask over my nose and mouth and I could breathe again. Then there was a confused period of time and movement, and finally we were out of the fog and fall of water, out of the burning warehouse and on the pier. The wind off the bay beat at me, made me shiver; the air in my lungs was cold and sweet. And I was seeing the huge lighted silhouette of the city's fireboat, *Phoenix,* lying just off the pier on the south side. That was where the heavy jet of water was coming from—one of the four big monitor nozzles mounted on her deck.

One of the squaddies was chattering into his walkie-talkie, telling somebody about me. Another asked if I could walk all right. I nodded, but he put an arm around my waist anyway— a good thing, because I needed the support. We went around the side of the warehouse, past other black-garbed men outfitted with Scott Paks and walkie-talkies, across bulging hoses to the front.

Frenetic scene out there: China Basin Street was clogged with pumpers, ladder trucks, support rigs; dozens of men running this way and that, shouting orders, laying down more hose, working the equipment. Two alarms, maybe three. Fireglow, glaring headlights and klieg lights, swirling red flashers; the pulsing drone of the pumpers, the thrum of the blaze, the sibilance of water from big ladder-pipe nozzles atop a pair of 100-foot aerials exploding into steam as it struck red-hot metal.

Other men converged on us as we appeared. A babble of voices, and more hands guiding me across the fire lines and out through the gate in the fence. They sat me down on the running board of an auxiliary truck drawn up in midstreet. I was shivering violently by then, still a little disoriented. Somebody put a rough blanket around my shoulders; somebody else gave me more oxygen, told me to breathe slowly and deeply. The oxygen cleared my head, eased some of the hurt in my chest. When I'd had enough I pushed the mask away. Then I was looking into the impending face of a big guy in a battalion chief's white hat.

"Okay now?" he asked.

"Okay."

"You need medical attention?"

"No."

"Sure?"

"I'm sure."

"What happened in there? How'd the fire start?"

I shook my head. I wasn't going to talk to him about that.

"The other man, the dead one . . . who is he?"

"Savarese. The owner."

"You work for him?"

"No."

"Then what were you doing in there?"

"Trying not to die," I said.

He looked at me hard for a couple of seconds; the fireshine reflected off the moisture on his face, made his features seem as hard as stone. Then he said, "Yeah," and hurried off toward the front lines.

Fire had claimed all of the warehouse now, throwing great cauliflowers of dirty smoke into the night sky. The air was wet with wind-blown mist off the half-dozen streams of water pouring from different angles into the building's shell. Part of the front wall and roof had already collapsed; the rest of it wouldn't last much longer. But the scurrying movement of men and equipment continued unchecked. Even though the boat club and salvage yard were some distance away on either side, there was still the threat of wind-carried cinders. Voices rose audibly here and there, hurling sentence fragments that had little or no meaning for me.

"Hold fast, hold fast!"

"That goddamn fence . . . can't lay any more spaghetti through there without risking a foul-up. . . ."

"Is that line charged? All right, haul it through. . . ."

"Stretch it over there! Stretch it!"

"Too late to knock it down now, even with a master stream. . . ."

I wondered if they'd gotten Savarese's corpse out—and less than a minute later I had the answer. Two squaddies carrying a black body bag appeared along the near side of the warehouse, brought it through the tangle of hoses that stretched through the fence. A white-outfitted paramedic joined them, took a look, moved away. The coroner's wagon wasn't there yet; they put what was left of Savarese down in the street.

Nobody was paying any attention to me.

I was no longer shaking; the blanket had insulated my sodden clothing from the wind. I got to my feet. My legs were still pretty wobbly, and there was a sharp, steady pain where the fragment of wood had burned my arm, and my chest kept producing hard little coughs. But I did not seem to have suffered any serious damage. I could get around all right.

I moved away from the auxiliary truck to where I had a better view up and down China Basin Street. Savarese's Plymouth van was no longer parked in front of the fence; the firefighters had moved it to make room for the pumpers and hoses—across and down the street, next to the network of old railroad spurs. As soon as I had it located I moved that way. I had to walk slow; when I tried to hurry my pace, the dizziness started up again.

The van was parked with the driver's door away from the fire. I went around on that side, leaned in across the seat. With the aid of the dome light I could see well enough to make a fast search of door pockets, glove box, seats, floor, and cargo space. There was not much to look at anyway, nothing that tied Savarese to Blackwell or did me any good. Blackwell was both shrewd and thorough; he'd been through the van before leaving here tonight, sure as hell, and he hadn't overlooked anything. The only lead I had to him was the credit card receipt I'd found under Savarese's desk blotter—and by this time it figured to be no lead at all.

I backed out, shut the door, started around to the front of the van. A shout went up from the firemen, and there was a concussive noise like a sonic boom that made the ground shudder under my feet. I turned in time to see spears of flame, great gouts of sparks and smoke boiling upward as the rest of the warehouse roof caved in on itself. Men ran toward and away from the heat and fallout, their eyes and minds fixed on what was happening inside.

I kept walking, not too fast, not letting myself think. My car was still parked where I'd left it in front of the boat club; I covered the distance to it unchallenged. Inside, I shed the blanket, started the engine and set the heater on high. When I could feel the warm air against my feet I put the car in gear, then swung in a tight U-turn around a red fire inspector's car before I switched on the headlights.

Farther down the street the police had set up barricades to keep the rubberneckers at bay. Out beyond, where China Basin Street hooks left to Third Street, hundreds of people were milling around, laughing, chattering, having a grand old time for themselves like celebrants at a pagan ritual. Bastards, I thought; I almost died in that frigging warehouse. But it was misdirected anger and I choked it down. One of the uniformed cops was gesturing for me to stop, and I did not want him to see what I was feeling.

He wanted to know who I was and where I was going. I gave him my name and a lie about taking myself to the emergency room. I'd been caught in the fire, I said, but I was all right to drive and the paramedics had told me to go ahead on my own. He thought about it. He could see I was telling the truth about being in the fire, and when I showed him the burn on my arm it made up his mind for him. He went and moved one of the barricades and let me through.

And that was a relief, because if he'd tried to detain me I don't know what I might have done to get free.

Chapter **19**

I DROVE STRAIGHT HOME. Not fast, not slow—safely.

It was the right place to go, the right thing to do, but I had to fight myself all the way. The dark, savage side of me wanted to go straight to Fisherman's Wharf, find out if the Harborside Inn was where Blackwell had been staying, see if he was still there . . . get my hands on him as fast as possible. But looking the way I did, nobody at the Harborside was going to tell me anything or allow me to wander the halls; and it was likely that Blackwell was long gone by now anyway, on his way south to the Salinas Valley. None of what he'd done tonight— torching the warehouse, killing Savarese, trying to kill me— made sense unless he knew or had a pretty good idea where Grady Haas could be found. So the most important thing for me to do was to call Arlo Haas, have him alert Constanza Vargas and her husband. After that, change clothes and do something about the burn on my arm. *Then* I would be ready to go hunting.

All the parking spaces near my building were filled; I left the car slanted across a neighbor's driveway, the hell with it.

There was no reason Blackwell would have come back here, be waiting inside my flat, but I unlocked the door cautiously and went in and through the place the same way. Kerry had tidied up before leaving; she never could stand a messy house. Kerry . . . ah Jesus, Kerry. I had another flash of her lying on the closet floor, and my throat closed up and the beast inside began yammering again to be let loose.

I couldn't remember Arlo Haas's telephone number. My pocket notebook was soggy, soot-stained, but I could read the number all right. I punched it out. Paced back and forth, waiting, because I could not remain still.

No answer.

Fifteen rings, twenty rings—no answer.

The bedside clock said that it was nearly half past midnight. Not much more than two hours since Blackwell had trapped me inside the warehouse office. Even if he'd left straight from there, even if he drove recklessly fast, he hadn't had enough time to get to San Bernado. He couldn't be the reason Haas was not answering his phone . . . or could he? Haas had been adamant about standing a twenty-four-hour watch on his property; a crisis involving Grady was the only thing that would have pried him loose from there, day or night. Some kind of telephone ruse by Blackwell? No. He didn't operate that way; his methods were sly, covert, sudden. If he knew about Haas and the farm, he'd go there and take the old man by surprise, just as he'd done with Bellin and Kerry and me.

So why wasn't Haas answering his phone at this late hour?

I called Monterey County information. There was a listing for Emilio Vargas on San Benito Street in San Lucas; a recorded voice gave me the number. But when I rang it all I got was some more empty circuit noise. Nobody home at the Vargas house either.

Something wrong down there . . .

I stripped off what was left of my wet clothes, kicked them into a corner. The burn on my arm was a hellish-looking thing, red and blistery and oozing. I ran cold water over it, dried it gently, pawed through the medicine cabinet and found a tube of something called Neosporin that Kerry must have bought and slathered that on. A wrapping of gauze, some adhesive, and then I washed my face and ran a comb through my hair, and all the while I was aware, like a harsh accelerated ticking in my mind, of the passage of time.

Bedroom, fresh clothes. *Tick, tick.* Another try at the Haas number, with the same results. *Tick, tick.* The Vargas number; still no answer. *Tick, tick, tick.*

And I was out of there.

BLACKWELL WAS A TORCH, a bug, a professional arsonist for hire.

He *had* to be, I thought as I drove the short distance to Fisherman's Wharf; everything pointed to it. Take any of the things that had happened, starting with the events of April Fools' Day, and you could explain it if Blackwell was a torch. Hell, you could explain Blackwell himself—his use of different names and addresses, his devious behavior, his cold-bloodedness. I'd done enough work for insurance companies, read enough literature put out by the arson department of the National Board of Fire Underwriters, to know that those tendencies were part of the psychological profile of most professional firebugs. They're the same breed as hit men for the Mob—amoral executioners who use fire instead of guns and who have the same disregard for human life. I remembered reading about one who'd been caught in Baltimore, a few years back, after setting a series of tenement fires. When the police told him seven people had died in those fires, he'd said, "So what?"

Everything about that blaze tonight smacked of bug work too. The explosion . . . some kind of ignition device using volatile chemicals or fulminants, with a timer to allow Blackwell to get well clear of the area. The speed in which the fire had spread indicated the use of boosters, "trailers," or both: kerosene or gasoline or solvent as an accelerant; a fast-burning substance such as wood shavings, excelsior, or cotton waste soaked in more fluid accelerant to run the fire in different directions. Amateurs don't set fires like that one tonight. It takes knowledge and skill.

Torches usually work for arson rings—tightly organized outfits that service well-insured business people who can't make a go of things and are open to a fast, lucrative, and unscrupulous way out. The rings operate almost solely on word of mouth advertising—one satisfied customer telling another. Some of the satisfied customers even work on a commission basis with a particular ring. The prospective new customer is put in contact with an intermediary, who works out the timing and other details and negotiates a price on behalf of the outfit's honchos. For the most part the torch's job is strictly to set fires, in such a way that they look like spontaneous combustion, accident, anything but what they really are. They seldom have any personal contact with the customer. The evident fact that in this case Blackwell had served as both intermediary and torch was uncommon but not unheard of. Could be something had happened to his ring's regular contact man—been arrested, fallen ill, died suddenly. Whatever the reason, Blackwell had been pressed into double duty.

I should have tumbled to the arson angle sooner, much sooner. All the signs of fire-for-hire were there: The small businessman with an old firetrap of a warehouse filled with an inflammable product that wasn't selling; bill collectors and his landlord hounding him, an ex-wife still putting on the squeeze, a tough-minded girlfriend who was tired of living on promises and figured to be making threats of her own. Prime fodder for the arson boys, that was Savarese. And then there were the meetings with Blackwell, and the things I'd found out about Blackwell, and Blackwell's monomaniacal hunt for Grady.

She was the reason for my shortsightedness. I'd been too focused on her, her actions, her emotional state, the danger she was in. She'd functioned—ironically enough—as a smoke-screen, obscuring the larger scheme in which she was nothing more than a by-product.

The general progression of events wasn't difficult to sort out now. April Fools' Day: Grady goes to Savarese Importing to investigate the damage claim Savarese had filed as a smoke-screen of his own. ("Hey, would I put in a claim for damaged goods if I was going to burn down my warehouse?") And she runs into Blackwell, either at the warehouse, where he's gone on some pretext to look the place over, or else somewhere in the vicinity. A spark of mutual attraction is struck, they start seeing each other, she falls in love with him—deeply, hope-lessly in love. And then something happens to burst the bub-ble. Maybe she sees or hears him talking to Savarese or some member of the arson ring about the torch job . . . something, in any case, that reveals her lover, her ideal man, to be a monster in disguise. It shatters her fragile interior. Either she confronts him and he shows her more of his true nature, or she simply packs up and flees the horror of her discovery. And one way or another he finds out that she's found out. And because that makes her a threat to both the Savarese job and his future, he sets out to find and silence her.

Had Savarese known about their affair, what had hap-pened to turn her from Blackwell's lover into his quarry? Pos-sible. But more likely, he hadn't known. More likely, he'd begun to get cold feet when I showed up asking questions; begun to fear getting caught, going to prison, and so tried to back out of the deal. Weak link, the kind that would break under police pressure. A third threat to Blackwell—to be elim-inated along with number two—was me. So Blackwell had used Savarese to set me up tonight, then put him down and out and left both of us to die in the fire.

Brutal, deadly—that was Blackwell the torch, the bug, the executioner. If he got his claws on Grady, he would kill her with the same swiftness and lack of compunction. Her and anybody else who happened to get in his way.

*   *   *

FISHERMAN'S WHARF. First time I'd been here in over a year, even though my flat is less than three miles away.

I remember the Wharf when it really was a fisherman's enclave. I remember it when most of the faces you saw were old-country Genovese and Sicilians, and most of the buildings housed wholesale fish dealers and boat builders and marine hardware outfits, and the wharves were piled high with rock cod and smelt and striped sea bass and huge quantities of fresh crab and bay shrimp. I remember it when the restaurants were few and the best in the city, and the streets were relatively clean, and there were no tourist facilities or cheap T-shirt and souvenir shops or sidewalk junk vendors or fast-food joints. I remember it when the pace was slow, the noise level tolerable, the air spicy with salt and fish and cooked crabs instead of foul with a mixture of exhaust fumes and frying grease. I remember Fisherman's Wharf when . . . and that's why I seldom go there anymore.

As late as it was—one-fifteen by my watch—the tourists were mostly tucked away in their beds and the streets were the domain of the night owls and the night predators. I had no trouble with snarled traffic or swarms of pedestrians, as I would have had in the daylight hours; and no trouble with parking, either, because the Harborside Inn—a smallish, ten-year-old pile of modernistic composition stone and glass—had its own underground garage.

I left my car with an attendant and went into a lobby done in tasteful greens and blues, with green-and-blue fishing murals on the walls. It was supposed to provide a Fisherman's Wharf ambiance. All it provided for me was an air of phoniness and hype.

The night clerk was a middle-aged woman wearing a blue suit and a green blouse and a blue-and-green scarf. I said to her, "I'm looking for a man named Blackwell. Is he registered here?"

"Blackwell. Just a moment, sir." There was a computer terminal at her fingertips; she poked at the keyboard, read the screen, gave me a spritely smile, and said, "No, sir, no Mr. Blackwell. Perhaps he hasn't checked in yet."

"How about a friend of his—King, Jack King?"

The computer again. And: "No, I'm sorry, no Mr. King."

"Man I'm looking for is about thirty-five, heavyset, short brown hair. Small curved scar under his right eye."

"Oh," she said immediately, "you mean Mr. *Queen.*"

"Queen," I said.

"Thomas Queen."

"I must have got the name mixed up," I said. "What room is Mr. Queen in?"

"I'm sorry, sir, but he's already checked out."

"When?"

"Earlier tonight."

"What time?"

"About ten-thirty, I think it was. He said he . . ."

But I was already moving away from her. Hurrying.

He'd found out about San Bernado, all right. And he was almost there by now, if he'd left the city at ten-thirty. But he couldn't know yet that Grady was staying in San Lucas . . . he *couldn't* know that, dammit.

There were public telephones near the lobby entrance to the bar. I used one of them to call the Vargas number and then Arlo Haas's number. Still nobody picked up at either place. Good and bad: If no one was home, then Blackwell couldn't get to Grady before I got to San Lucas. But why wasn't anybody home? And what if somebody came back at the wrong time and found the executioner waiting?

Chapter **20**

DESPITE THE LATENESS of the hour, I had some traffic to contend with between the city and San Jose. It forced me to hold my speed down to sixty-five, just to be safe. Chilly night at that end of the bay, too; I drove with the window down, and the cold air rushing against my face helped keep fatigue at bay. So did the radio, turned up loud to a country-and-western station. So did the burn on my arm.

Just south of San Jose, I stopped for gas and again tried calling Arlo Haas and the Vargases. Still no answers.

Once I got clear of the San Jose city limits, there was hardly any traffic at all. It was nearly three by then. I upped my speed, but only to a little better than seventy-five; the car was twenty years old and the engine had a lot of miles on it and there was a bad shimmy when you pushed the speed up past eighty. My mind had been working steadily, worrying at things, but after a while it began to shut down little by little, until I wasn't thinking much at all. Just driving. Watch the road, feel the bite of the wind and the burn pain, hear the drone of the disc jockey's voice and the loud, twangy beat of the music. Just driving.

Slow down coming into Salinas and passing through. Pick up speed again at the southern outskirts. Empty highway again for the most part; the occasional headlights were like sudden eyes in the night, glaring at you and then gone.

Down near Chualar there was a spasming in my chest, a fit of coughing that left my lungs feeling hot and raw. Otherwise, there were no residual effects from the smoke I'd inhaled—not yet, anyway.

Gonzales, Soledad, Greenfield . . . little towns, blotches of light in the darkness, come and gone. My eyes were gritty, my head ached from the strain of night driving. Static on the radio; the country station was fading out. Fiddle with the dial, find another station—fifties and sixties rock music this time. Somebody singing "Hang On, Sloopy." Yeah. All you got to do is *hang on.*

King City. Watch it through here. Big Highway Patrol substation in King City and the area had a reputation as a speed trap. I slowed down, and a good thing I did. One of the patrol cruisers passed me heading north, and in the rearview mirror I saw the driver slacken his speed a little; he didn't turn and come after me, but he might have if I'd been traveling any faster. That was all I'd need now, this close: get stopped, get a ticket, get delayed.

South of King City, then, into the southern end of the valley and the last leg to San Lucas. Empty landscape, faintly silvered under a pale, cloud-edged moon, the foothills shining like great mounds of dough lightly dusted with flour. Bleak at this hour, desolate, remote. Big gusty wind blowing over the valley, raising plumes and swirls of dust, making the trees tremble as if in fear. False illusion: a lunar landscape, a dead place where nothing grew, nothing lived. And where's all your sentiment now, smart guy? All gone, blown away by the dark wind.

Just a few miles to go to San Lucas. But a lot more than
that to go before I got any rest, any peace . . .

THE PORCH LIGHT was on at the Vargas house. No
other lights, but I could see only part of the house as I pulled
up next to the sagging fence. Somebody was home, though, if
the two other cars parked there meant anything—the old
Chrysler Imperial and the rust-infested pickup I'd seen on my
last visit.

I got out into the rough wind. Muscles stiff, back hurting,
the scraped feeling still in my chest. Old man, I thought. Some
match for Blackwell when I find him. And him with a gun. All
I had was a full load of righteous anger. Blow him away with
that, all right.

I'm a damned fool, I thought.

Through the gate, past the patch of prickly pear—twisted
shapes in the darkness, like appendages piled up in a mad
surgeon's yard—and onto the porch. I found the doorbell,
worked it. A little time passed, and I rang the bell some more
and hammered on the panel with my fist, and a little more
time passed, and then the door opened, fast, and I was looking
down the bore of a rifle. The heavy-bellied man holding it said
in a hard, angry voice, *"Qué pasa, hombre?"*

Before I could answer, Constanza Vargas appeared alongside the man. Like him, she was wearing pajamas and a robe—
but neither of them looked as though they had been asleep.
She said something to him in rapid Spanish that had my name
in it. He answered her in Spanish; then he lowered the rifle,
almost but not quite all the way down, and said to me in
English, "Eight hours we been waiting. Where you been all
that time?" He was still angry.

There was nothing to say to that; I didn't know what he
meant. I said, "Grady—is she asleep?"

The two of them exchanged looks. "No," Constanza Vargas said, "she didn't come back."

". . . She's not here? Where did she go?"

"We don't know." She shook her head wearily. "We just got home an hour ago."

"Where were you? Out looking for her?"

For some reason that clouded her husband up even more. "You know where we were, man."

Mrs. Vargas said, "Emilio," in a gentling voice and stepped around him. "Come inside," she said to me, and reached out to pluck at my coat sleeve. "It's cold out there, we can talk better inside."

I went in past Emilio Vargas, who gave ground grudgingly. Too cold outside, too warm inside. The room we went into felt as humid as a bathroom after somebody has finished taking a long, hot shower; they must have had the heat up over seventy. I started to sweat immediately inside my heavy overcoat.

The woman invited me to sit down. I told her I preferred to stand. She nodded and seated herself on an overstuffed chair under an oil painting of one of the missions. Her husband stood stolidly near the doorway; he still held the rifle but now the muzzle was pointed at the floor. In here, in the stronger light, I could see that both of them were as fatigued as I was, Mrs. Vargas solemn-eyed and anxious, her husband nursing a measure of exasperation along with his anger.

I asked, "When did Grady leave here?"

"I told you," Constanza Vargas said. "In the afternoon."

"You didn't tell me. What time in the afternoon?"

"Between four and five o'clock. Emilio had not come home yet and I was making dinner. The last I saw of her, she was sitting in the backyard."

"She take anything with her, clothing or anything?"

"No. Only her purse."

"Just went away, no word?"

"Only the note to you."

"To me?"

"It was on the table by her chair, outside."

"What did it say?"

"I will get it for you."

She stood, hurried out of the room. In the hot silence that followed her exit, Emilio Vargas watched me with his dark, wrathful eyes. The twitchiness was in me and I wanted to pace; instead I stayed put, shifting my weight from one foot to the other, sweating.

I said to Vargas, "I've been trying to call Grady's father all night. He doesn't answer his phone. You have any idea why?"

Silence. Then, with a little puzzlement, "What's the matter with you, man? You gone loco?"

"What kind of answer is that?"

"Maybe that's why you didn't come to the hospital, huh?"

"Hospital?"

"All night we waited. Constanza said you'd come. You told her you would."

"I told her . . . ?"

Constanza Vargas was coming back into the room, but that was not why I stopped talking. I was beginning to get it, what this conversation was all about, why Emilio Vargas was so upset, some of what had happened down here last night.

Mrs. Vargas glanced at me, at her husband; reached out and put a piece of paper in my hand. I didn't look at it. I said, "Arlo Haas is in the hospital. Is that it?"

Frowning, she said, "In Paso Robles, yes. But . . ."

"What happened to him?"

"It was as we feared."

"Another stroke?"

"Yes."

"Last night sometime. At his house."

"Yes."

"What time last night?"

"*Cristo!*" her husband said. "You *must* be loco. She told you all that on the phone."

"Not me, she didn't."

"But . . . I did," Mrs. Vargas said. "I called you, I spoke to you . . ."

"My home number—that's the one you called?"

"Yes."

"What time?"

"Seven o'clock. Not long after Emilio and I found Mr. Haas and called for the ambulance. Your business card, it was by his telephone. I wanted you to know what had happened. . . ."

Blackwell, I thought. That's how he found out about San Bernado. Phong rang while he was searching my flat and the brazen bastard picked right up and grunted something and Constanza Vargas thought she was talking to me. Why wouldn't she? It was my number and she didn't know my voice very well and she was rattled to begin with.

I explained that to the Vargases, briefly, without mentioning Kerry. Confusion and color both faded out of the woman's face, leaving it pinched, haggard. *"Madre de Dios,"* she said. "Then he knows . . . he will come here. . . ."

"If he does," Emilio Vargas said, lifting the rifle, "he will go away without his head."

I asked Mrs. Vargas, "What did you tell him on the phone? Did you give him your name?"

"Yes."

"Your husband's name? Mention San Lucas?"

"No. No."

"Does Mr. Haas have an address book in his house—anything that might contain your address and telephone number?"

"I don't remember seeing one . . . no, I don't think so."

"All right. Then the man who's after Grady doesn't know where to find you, not yet; you can't be the only Vargases in the county directory. He may try to call here, ask for you by name. If he does that, you don't know who Constanza Vargas is. Play dumb, don't tell him anything."

"I will answer the phone if it rings," her husband said darkly. His anger burned even hotter now, with a new target to focus it on. He patted his rifle. "And I will answer the door with this—"

"No," I said, "don't open up for anybody." He started to argue, so I turned away from him, asked his wife, "What else did you tell the man on the phone? Try to remember exactly what you said."

I watched her work her memory. "I told him . . . 'Mr. Haas has had another stroke and the ambulance is on the way.' I said we—my husband and I—we would go with him to the hospital in Paso Robles."

"Paso Robles . . . you named the town?"

"Yes."

"And the man? What did he say?"

"He asked if Grady was there too."

"And you told him no."

Nod. "I said I don't know where she is, she went away between four and five o'clock. I told him about the note."

"What did he say to that?"

"Only that he would come to the hospital as soon as he could."

"Anything else?"

"No. Then he hung up."

He hadn't wanted to say too much, I thought. She might have realized he wasn't me. She'd already told him enough so that he could find his way down here and continue the hunt on his own hook—pinpoint where Arlo Haas and Constanza Vargas lived, maybe stake out the hospital in Paso Robles on the chance that Grady would show up there.

I asked, "What's Mr. Haas's condition?"

"Not good. *Ay de mí,* not good."

"The doctors think he'll live?"

"They don't know yet," Emilio Vargas said. "If he does live, he might not walk again."

"Was he able to speak when you found him?"

"He spoke, but we couldn't understand what he said."

"So you don't know what brought on the stroke."

"No."

"Why'd you go to his farm?"

"I tried to telephone him," Constanza Vargas said, "to tell him Grady was gone, but he didn't answer. Three times I called. When Emilio came home from work we drove there to find out what was wrong."

For the first time I looked at the piece of paper she'd put in my hand. Small sheet of blue notepaper. Grady's neat, precise handwriting in dark blue ink. My name as the salutation.

I have been thinking about what you said, and of course you're right. He might find his way here and I mustn't take any chances that my father or the Vargases will be harmed. Please don't try to find me. Please let me do what I have to do. Yours very truly, Grady Haas

Christ, I thought. She's going back to the city, back home to make it easy for him; and when he comes, she'll surrender herself like a sacrificial lamb. That's what this is all about—a form of suicide. Death on the altar of what she perceives as an unholy love.

I put the note in my coat pocket. "Grady left here on foot, is that right? Didn't take any form of transportation that you know about?"

Mrs. Vargas shook her head. "She must have walked away."

"And then hitchhiked, I suppose. She'd be able to do that around here, wouldn't she?"

"Someone would give her a ride, yes."

To her father's farm; that was the obvious place. Maybe then she'd told Haas she was going away, back home—maybe that was what had triggered his stroke. But if that was it, the attack hadn't come until later, when he was alone. She wouldn't have gone away and left him if she'd known he was suffering, maybe dying. She wasn't *that* bereft inside.

"Grady's car," I said. "Was it still at the farm, still inside the barn?"

"We didn't look," Emilio Vargas said. "When we found the old man . . . all we thought about was him."

His wife asked me, "You think she went there for her car?"

"Makes more sense than trying to hitchhike out of the valley."

"But then where would she go?"

I shook my head.

"Not to San Francisco?"

"No," I lied, "not to San Francisco."

"That man . . . you don't think he has already . . ."

"Found Grady? No. He hasn't had enough time."

"Who is he? Why is he after her?"

"I don't know," I lied again. "She's the only one who does."

"Then how will you find him, stop him?"

I didn't answer that. I'd had enough talk; and the heat in there was becoming intolerable. Sweat ran on my body. My mind felt muzzy, the way it does when you have a fever. But there was one more thing that needed to be said.

I asked Emilio Vargas, "You have another weapon in the house besides that rifle?"

"No."

"Not even a target pistol? I'm unarmed."

Headshake. "I would give it to you if I did."

"All right."

I moved past them, out to the front entrance. They followed. As I opened the door and went into the windy dark, Constanza Vargas said behind me, *"Vaya con Dios,"* in a voice that made the words sound like a prayer. I didn't respond. But the phrase stayed with me into the car, most of the way out of San Lucas. *Vaya con Dios.* Go with God.

No, I thought, no. God has nothing to do with this. With most things, maybe, but not with everything on this earth. And not with this.

Chapter **21**

CATTLEMEN ROAD WAS DESERTED; I didn't meet another car between San Lucas and the turnoff to the Haas farm. When I neared the side road that snaked back into the hills to the gravel company, I shut off my headlights and slowed to twenty-five. The moon was still out and the sky above the eastern foothills was just beginning to show the first seepage of dawn. I could make out the road and the surrounding terrain all right.

I eased onto Haas's farm lane through the open gate, up atop the railroad right-of-way. From there the shapes of the house and outbuildings were visible against the hill folds. All of them were dark. But that didn't mean anything one way or another. If Blackwell was there, waiting, he wouldn't have the lights blazing at this hour. Not him. He spun his webs in the dark.

Where the windbreak of eucalyptus started, I swung off the lane and put the car in behind the trees. I took the flashlight with me when I got out. The wind was strong here, redolent of earth and sage and grapevines; it chilled my face as I hurried along the edge of the road where the tree-shadow was thickest. The early-morning dark seemed alive with sound, but most of it was created by the wind: rustlings and rattlings in the eucalyptus, in the vineyard rows beyond; groaning creaks from the tumbledown fence across the way; birdlike flappings from the blown tails of my overcoat; moans, whispers, little purling cries. Listen to the wind, especially at night, and you can hear all the sounds a human being makes—and some that no human would ever want to utter.

I kept thinking about Blackwell, trying to put myself in his skin. What had he done when he got down here tonight? Two possibilities, given what he knew and what he didn't know. Start tracking Grady immediately; find out Haas's address from a telephone directory, come here to the farm, search the place, wait or move on to Paso Robles or try to locate the Vargases. Or else get himself a motel room, catch a few hours' sleep, and start fresh at daybreak. He spun his webs in the dark, sure, but he was also cautious, methodical. And as far as he knew, I was cooked as crisp as Savarese—so nobody was chasing him, there was no longer any real urgency in finding and disposing of Grady. Those facts argued in favor of the motel possibility. On the other side of the ledger, he knew Grady had disappeared again and he wouldn't want her to get too much of a jump on him. And he couldn't be sure of how much Arlo Haas and the Vargases knew about him, what Grady or I might have told them.

Toss-up, take your pick: I could see him doing it either way. I'd know which one, or at least have a better idea of which one, when I got to the house.

I wished again that Emilio Vargas had had a gun for me. I wished again that I didn't have such a fundamental aversion to handguns, that I had bought one of my own for times like this. I wished again that I wasn't a damned fool.

Fifty yards from the barn now. And I was aware of a new sound, rising above the others: the irregular, ratchety rhythm of the old windmill. Like the beat of a bad heart. Like the beginnings of a death rattle. In spite of the cold I was sweating again—as if the tight-winding of my body was squeezing moisture out through the pores.

The last of the trees grew just beyond where the lane ended and the farmyard began; I crept up behind its bole to reconnoiter. No car in the yard, or on the extension of the farm road past the house, or anywhere else within the range of my vision. No movement at the house or barn. I waited until clouds crawled across the pale moon; ran in a low crouch and at an angle to the rear of the barn, then along the back wall to the far side. Nothing to see or hear over there, either.

I followed the side wall, went around and along the front wall to the double doors. Got one half open and slipped inside. Heavy darkness. I was alone in it; you get so you can sense another person's presence in closed places like that. I shielded the flashlight with my hand and switched it on—just long enough to see that the only car there was the older Ford with the Handicapped Driver placard on the dash. Grady had been here to collect her Geo, all right. The question was—when?

I opened the barn door again, looked out. Windy dark— but not quite as dark now; the shapes of things were beginning to take on more definition. Dawn wasn't far off. He's not here, I thought. Been here, maybe, but not here now. Still, I went out carefully, and when I crossed to the archway in the lattice fence I did it in a hard run.

The barking started before I was halfway across. Gus, the black Lab; I'd forgotten about him. He was somewhere inside the house, at the back, and he stayed there as I came up onto the porch. The Vargases must have shut him into one of the rear rooms, whichever one contained his food and water dishes.

I stood by the door for half a minute, listening to the dog and the wind. The door was locked, but it wasn't much of a lock; I had it open in another half-minute. I was still on sharp alert when I entered, but the feel in there was the same as in the barn. Gus and I had the place to ourselves.

This time I used my handkerchief to shield the flashlight lens before I flicked it on. The old-fashioned parlor was on the right; I went in there first. The shades were drawn and there were the smells of dog and old meals eaten alone. One of the cushions from Haas's rocking chair was on the floor and the rocker itself was skewed out of position. Blackwell? Or was this where Haas had had his stroke?

At the back of the house, now, the Lab was alternately barking and whining. I could also hear the agitated click of his nails, on the floor and scratching against a door panel. I felt sorry for him. He was alone and caged-in and he didn't under- stand what was going on; and that made him nervous, scared. Same way a human would feel in a similar situation. Haas had told me he didn't bite, but I'm not much with dogs and it wouldn't do him any good if I let him roam the house. I wasn't the one he wanted to see anyway.

I took a fast turn around the parlor, switching the flash on and off to guide me. Nothing other than the rocker appeared to have been disturbed. Across a central hall, then, and into the dining room on the opposite side. The first time I flicked on the light I didn't see anything to hold my attention. But the second time, deeper into the room, I did notice something.

On the dining-room table were three coffee cups in three saucers, each before a different chair. I moved over for a closer look. The three cups made me think of Papa Bear, Mama Bear, and Baby Bear: one was empty, one was half full, and the other was full to the brim. The half-full cup had a stain of something on the rim. I bent, laid the beam up close to it.

Lipstick. Plum-colored lipstick.

Mary Ellen Crowley, I thought.

Three cups; three people. Mary Ellen and Haas—and Grady. Early yesterday evening, because Haas was a neat man and the cups wouldn't still be here if he'd had enough time to remove them to the kitchen. The three of them, having coffee here together. . . .

Sure, I thought, sure. Grady didn't hitchhike out of San

Lucas; she wasn't the type to call on strangers for anything if she could avoid it. No, she'd walked from the Vargas house to that little grocery in San Lucas and she'd called her old friend Mary Ellen Crowley and asked Mary Ellen to pick her up and drive her here to the farm. And when they got here they'd had coffee with Haas—at Mary Ellen's urging, probably. And then what? Had Grady announced that she was leaving, returning to San Francisco? They would have tried to talk her out of it, if so, but to no avail. In any case she'd got her car out of the barn and drove off, and Mary Ellen had left too. And a short while later—not too long or Haas would have tried to call me at home, to tell me about Grady leaving—the strain had brought on his stroke.

If Grady had driven back to the city last night she'd be at her apartment now, right? I returned to the parlor, to the table where Haas kept his phone. No address book of any kind in the drawer. And I hadn't written Grady's number down when I was in her apartment, because I hadn't thought I'd need it. If it wasn't listed . . . But it was. San Francisco information gave it to me, and I rang it.

Circuit noise, nothing else.

So was she there and just not answering her phone? Or not there? Could be the scenario I'd worked out wasn't quite right and she hadn't gone to San Francisco last night after all. Had another destination in mind that she'd let slip to her old school chum, Mary Ellen.

There was a local telephone directory in the table drawer; I hauled it out, looked up Mary Ellen Crowley. No listing for her or anybody named Crowley in the area. Unlisted number, if she had a phone at all. Damn people and their idiosyncrasies!

Constanza Vargas, I thought. She might know where Mary Ellen lived. I punched out the Vargas number, and pretty soon her husband answered with the anger still sharp in his voice. Yes, he would ask Constanza about Mary Ellen Crowley. No, no one else had called and no one had come around their house. Better not, he said grimly. He went away for half a minute, and when he came back on the line he said, "She doesn't know."

I waited until he'd disconnected before I banged the receiver down. Gus had quit barking; now he was whining pitifully and the sounds were like an irritant on my raw nerves. Did Haas have Mary Ellen's address and/or telephone number written down anywhere in the house? Better look. He might have the other thing I needed too.

I climbed the stairs to the second floor, combed through his bedroom. Nothing. A second bedroom had once been Grady's and it had been left as it was when she'd last lived here—full of a girl's things, a girl's mementoes, all of them abandoned when she began her new adult life in San Francisco. Nothing there for me. Nor in any of the other three upstairs rooms.

No addresses or telephone numbers.

And no handgun. Just his twelve-gauge, down in the parlor, but that was too unwieldy to be of much use to me away from here.

Well? Now what? Blackwell hadn't been here yet; I was reasonably sure of that. Wait for him? Hide my car in the barn and take him by surprise when he showed? It sounded good, but what if he *didn't* show? What if his first move this morning —or even last night—had been to go down to Paso Robles and stake out the hospital? And what if he decided to hang out there the whole damn day? I'd go crazy waiting here, not knowing where Grady was, not knowing if things were happening elsewhere. I needed to move and keep on moving until I had more answers—some sense of where people were and what they were doing.

Downstairs, out of the house into the breaking dawn, with Gus's canine laments in my ears and fatigue and the sense of urgency eating at me like lye. I was walking when I started across the yard, trotting by the time I reached the eucalyptus, running before I was halfway to where I'd left my car.

Squirrel in a wheel: running fast, but where the hell was I going?

THE SUN WAS CREEPING UP from behind the foothills when I reached San Bernado. The only business establishment open at this hour was the café where I'd eaten lunch on Monday. The place was already three-quarters full: Mexican farm workers, mostly, and a couple of truck drivers.

I took the last stool at the counter. I was so tired, and wound up so tight, that I felt groggy. The food smell was doing things to my stomach, too; I hadn't eaten in close to twenty-four hours. I ordered coffee and two sugar doughnuts, and when the waitress brought them I asked her if she knew where Mary Ellen Crowley lived. The name didn't mean anything to her, not even when I added that Mary Ellen taught at the union school. Cook would probably know, she said and rolled her eyes; he knew *everything*. Turned out he did know: Mary Ellen Crowley lived in San Ardo, not San Bernado—ten miles down the road. He was sure of that, but not of the street. Hollister, he thought it might be. He had no idea of the number.

Squirrel in a wheel . . .

I ate the doughnuts too fast, drank a second cup of coffee the same way, and got back into the car and back on the road. San Ardo was a little larger than San Bernado, but with the same musty, dusty, time-snagged look and feel. The first place I came to that was open was a service station; I pulled in there and talked to the attendant, who looked as if he hadn't been long out of a union school himself. Mary Ellen Crowley? Oh sure, he said, she lived on Hollister Street, big brown house in the second block, two plum trees in the front yard. She and her husband and their little girl. What you did, you drove down Main Street two blocks and turned left. . . .

I drove down Main Street two blocks and turned left, and I was on Hollister Street. The big brown house with the two plum trees had a pair of cars parked in the driveway, neither of which I'd ever seen before. The unpaved street in front was empty.

As early as it was, I thought I might have to make some noise to get the Crowleys out of bed. But I only had to ring the bell once. In five seconds flat the door opened and I was look-ing at Mary Ellen herself, wearing a bathrobe but wide-awake and with her hair hastily combed. She wore an expectant look until she recognized me; then it was replaced by one of sur-prise and puzzlement.

"Why . . . the detective," she said. "How did you know?"

"Know what?"

"That Grady was here."

". . . I didn't know," I said. "She's not here now?"

"No. But you didn't miss her by much."

"She spent the night with you?"

"Yes. She didn't want to but I talked her into it." Mary Ellen glanced over her shoulder and then came out onto the porch and shut the door behind her. "My daughter and my husband are still in bed," she said. "I don't want to wake them."

"What time did Grady leave?"

"Not more than twenty minutes ago. When you rang the bell I thought she'd changed her mind and come back."

"She say where she was going?"

"To see her father and then back to San Francisco. I spent most of last night trying to talk her out of that. Going home, I mean."

"To the farm first? You're sure?"

"Yes. We were there yesterday; she called me from San Lucas and asked me to pick her up. . . ."

"I know," I said. "Go on."

"Well, not long after we arrived she told Mr. Haas she'd decided to go back to the city. He got angry and she ran out. I went after her, convinced her to come home with me. We had dinner and talked—I talked, mostly—and by then it was late and she agreed to spend the night. But this morning she was just as determined to go home to the city. She . . . Lord, I don't know what's happened to her. She's like a zombie."

"She wouldn't confide in you?"

"No. She simply won't talk about it."

"Was it her idea to stop at the farm this morning?"

"No, it was mine. I made her promise. She owes her father that much. He was so angry and upset yesterday . . ."

"Too angry and upset," I said. "He had another stroke after you two left."

Her face went pale. "Oh my God," she said. "He's not . . . ?"

"No. Constanza Vargas and her husband found him and called an ambulance. He's in the hospital in Paso Robles."

"But Grady . . . she has to know. When she gets to the farm and finds he's not there, she won't know what to think."

"Try calling her there," I said. "If she answers tell her to come back here right away, you want to go with her to Paso Robles. Then keep her here until you hear from me. Will you do that?"

"Yes, of course, but I don't understand what—"

"I'll explain later." I was already moving down off the porch.

"Where are you going?" she called after me.

"To the farm. In case Grady doesn't answer the phone."

HER CAR, the light blue Geo Storm, was parked in the farmyard. I saw it from atop the railroad right-of-way, and because I didn't see any other car I kept on going up the farm lane and into the yard. Rolled to a stop behind the Geo.

When I got out I could hear the wild wind and Gus barking in the house and nothing else. The front door of the house was standing wide open. I ran over there and inside, calling Grady's name. The dog's barking got louder; that was my only response. I swept through the downstairs rooms, all but the

kitchen, where Gus was, and then did the same with the upstairs rooms. She wasn't there.

Outside again, I looked into the Geo. Her purse was on the
passenger seat and the keys were in the ignition. I reached in,
took the keys; then I ran across to the barn and poked my
head inside. Empty. I stood in the yard and yelled her name,
but that didn't buy me anything either.

Where the hell was she?

The hills? Walking in the hills?

The thought was chilling and at first I rejected it. Comes
back here this morning, finds the house empty, no sign of her
father, doesn't have a clue of where he is or what might have
happened to him, and instead of telephoning Constanza Vargas, instead of waiting, she wanders off into the goddamn hills?
She wouldn't really do something like that, would she?

Then I remembered how much time she'd spent in those
hills as a child and since she'd returned to the valley, and the
way she'd looked and talked in San Lucas, and the things
she'd done before and since, and Mary Ellen Crowley saying,
"She's like a zombie," and I thought: Yeah, she would. It's just
what she'd do.

I fired up my car, swung it around the Geo and over onto
the extension of the farm road that curved up the hillside beyond the house. The roadbed was rocky, heavily rutted, the
earth loose in the ruts, and I had to go slow to maintain trac-
tion on the climb. Finally I nosed over the crest to where I
could see down the opposite slope.

The hair crawled on my neck. I was suddenly cold outside,
hot and tight inside.

Car on the downslope, drawn up at an angle near the bottom, blocking passage.

Dark brown Buick.

Blackwell.

Chapter **22**

I PUT THE BRAKES ON HARD and slewed to a stop ten yards from the Buick's rear bumper. There was nobody inside it that I could see, nobody around it, nobody anywhere in the vicinity. I bounced out, ran ahead past the Buick. Below it the road made a dogleg to the right and ended in a mostly flat area the size of a couple of football fields. Cattle graze once, Arlo Haas had told me. Now it was scattered clumps of sage and patches of dry, brown grass like ragged beard stubble and rocky, ash-colored earth—dead ground, as if a plague of some kind had swept over it and left it devastated. Void of human life, too, as were the windswept hillsides surrounding it. No Grady, no Blackwell.

I ran back to the Buick, thinking: She got here, went for her walk, then he showed and saw her car and hunted in the house for her and then drove on over here, all the same as I did. Left his car because he didn't want to risk getting it stuck out on the flat. But did he see her first or go tracking blind? And how long ago?

The driver's door on the Buick was closed, but only on

half-latch; I yanked it open, bent inside. The dash compartment contained nothing but a rental-company folder. The single item on the seats was a man's trenchcoat, in back. I caught it up, shook it, felt the pockets; empty. Trunk release, a quick look back there. Spare tire and a leather suitcase. I ripped the case open, pawed through it. No weapon of any kind. Whatever firepower he had, he was carrying with him.

I opened up the trunk of my car. All I kept in there that would serve as a weapon was a bow-shaped tire iron. I dragged that out and set off running again, out onto the flat.

There weren't any footprints for me to follow; the ground was too rocky and dry, too well scoured by the wind. So I had no way of telling if either of them had gone straight across or climbed the bare hillsides or veered off onto a barely discernible track—once a cowpath, probably—that angled into a crease on my left. I hesitated, trying to decide which route to take. The cowpath . . . it was closer and at the least it would take me to other vantage points.

The path was only a couple of feet wide through the crease, twice that on the other side. The swelling folds of the hills hemmed it in, so I had limited visibility ahead. Overhead, to the north, a hawk flew in slow, gliding circles, black and two-dimensional against the bright sky; there was no other movement. The sage-heavy wind made the only sounds, now loud, now soft; never silent. You couldn't have heard a human voice shouting more than fifty yards away.

Down into a dry creekbed, across and up the other side. The sharp urgency kept prodding me and I wanted to run, but the ground was uneven and I didn't want to take the chance of falling, twisting an ankle. There was a kind of vibrating weakness in my legs, a cinderlike grittiness that played tricks with my vision. Fatigue . . . the weight of it growing heavier by the minute. I was no longer thinking with complete clarity. But for now that was all right. This was not a time for thinking.

I'd gone about a hundred yards when a little rise came up

ahead; the track climbed it and so did I. No sign of Grady or
Blackwell on the far side, but another thirty or forty yards
distant I could make out something else: a wood and barbed
wire boundary fence that ran in a drunken line up the hillside
on my right. Beyond the fence was an open area—ravine,
gorge, something like that. The upper and lower parts of it
were hidden by the configuration of the terrain.

Another twenty slogging yards, and the opening beyond
the fence began to take on shape and contours. It wasn't a
ravine or gorge at all; it was man-made—a deep, wide,
U-shaped cut in the hillside. When I reached the fence I looked
down a long bare-rock slope into about two-thirds of the pit,
all the way to the bottom. Road down there, leading in from
the west; and earth-moving equipment, and a couple of big
dump trucks, and a rock crusher and a network of jutting
conveyers stretched out to mounds of gravel, and a few small
tin-roofed buildings. Up along the two visible sides of the U
were rough-graded roadbeds and terraced shelves containing
more earth-moving equipment.

Quarry. South Valley Gravel Company.

From this vantage point I couldn't make out any people or
activity. Just the big Cats and skiploaders and trucks, like
orange and gray creatures at rest in some prehistoric pit.
Union outfit, probably: shut down for the weekend.

Even if there was a way down from here, I doubted Grady
would use it. The quarry was private property and she'd shun
any possible contact with strangers; and it wasn't her kind of
place anyway, with all that heavy equipment. Across the flat
was where she must have gone, her and Blackwell both.

Now I had even more impetus to run, and I might have
except that when I turned from the fence I was looking uphill
and something caught my eye—movement along the upper
rim of the cut. I froze, squinting because the sun was up that
way and its glare was dazzling. I had to rub grit out of my eyes
before I could tell that there was somebody up there, one per-

son moving toward the edge, then stopping behind some kind of low rise in the ground.

Grady, that long black hair of hers whipping in the wind.

And then a second figure, a man, Blackwell, came into view and stopped a few feet away from her.

For a little time none of us moved. Me down here, the two of them above, braced against the buffeting wind not ten feet from a short, steep incline like the brow of a forehead; and below that incline a sheer drop of eighty or ninety feet down the quarry's scarred upper wall to one of the graded shelves.

There were more than a hundred yards separating me from them, all of it uphill. I started to run along the fence; there was nothing else I could do. The wind was gusting, blowing loud as well as hard, and a shout at this distance was no better than a whisper. I ran out in the open, waving both my arms when I didn't have to use the tire iron to help maintain my balance. I wanted to be seen, I wanted Blackwell to know I was alive and coming for him. It would take his attention away from her.

But it didn't happen that way. He had his back to me, and if she saw me—and she must have, at least peripherally—she did not react or say anything to him, because he didn't turn his body or his head. They kept standing in place, gazes locked, her with her arms down flat against her sides, him with his hands fisted on his hips. But there was nothing good in the frozen tableau; he was not having second thoughts about killing her, or even nerving himself up to doing it. Not him—not the executioner. Saying something to her, maybe telling her matter-of-factly why he was about to take her life. And her standing stiff and soul-dead, Little Miss Selfish, Little Miss Stupid, waiting, no fight in her, no resistance, just waiting passively for him to put an end to her misery.

The angle of ascent and the footing weren't too bad at first; I was able to scramble along at a good clip, now and then digging the tire iron into the earth to keep from slipping. My grip on the iron was slick with sweat. Sweat encased my body, too, crawled under the bandage on my arm and made the burned flesh sting. I was aware of all that, and of the wind, and of the black hatred seething like acid inside me.

I came up over a humped section of ground, onto a short gradual slope. The boundary fence hooked toward me at that point, ran through a narrow fold between two rounded mounds, close-set, like ashy brown, nippleless breasts. I scaled the fence, snagging the tail of my coat on a strand of barbed wire, ripping it free with only one lost step. They were out of sight then, for the fifteen or twenty seconds it took me to climb the nearest of the mounds; and when I reached the crest and saw them again, he was moving toward her. Not fast, not slow —deliberately.

She held her position. Stood very still, hair aswirl, eyes fixed on his face, and let him come.

I was nearly parallel to the top of the cut, directly below where they were. The slope that parted us now was not steep, and there were less than fifty yards of it. I half-ran, half-slid down the mound and got my legs under me and plowed up the slope, my mouth open to yell so Blackwell would hear me. But I was short of breath and the wind took the sounds I made and tore them apart.

He stopped again up there, close to her. And looked into her face for two or three beats. And then he hit her—closed fist, a short solid blow on the point of the jaw. She crumpled, but he caught her before she went all the way down. Effort-lessly, he swung her up into his arms. Then he started toward the foot-high earth wrinkle separating the edge of the hilltop from the incline and the quarry below.

Something happened inside me, a kind of tearing. My chest heaved, a roaring came out of my throat that overrode the whistling clamor of the wind.

"Blackwell!"

He heard it. And he quit moving, came to a jerky halt five feet from the edge; swiveled half-around to stare downslope. I'd covered half the fifty yards and was closing fast, and I could see his face clearly, the recognition and stunned disbelief that held him rooted, the sudden warping of his features as anger and fear and animal self-preservation took hold.

Less than twenty yards . . . and he dropped Grady. Didn't put her down, just spread his arms and let go of her limp body. She fell jarringly at his feet. He stepped over her, digging into the pocket of the light jacket he wore. But the wind had got under the jacket, filled and inflated it around him, and he had a little trouble getting his gun out, just enough so that I was able to cross another few feet of ground. Then he had the piece in his hand, a small automatic, and was bringing it to bear, and there were still ten yards between us and I knew he would fire before I covered half that distance.

I threw the tire iron at him.

Did it without thinking, just lifted my arm and threw it. He saw it coming, tried to dodge and shoot me at the same time, only his foot slipped and he overcompensated and stepped right into the path of the iron. The gun went off . . . wild shot, nowhere near me . . . and the tire iron hit him on the right forearm with enough force that even above the wind I heard the crack of bone, then his thin piercing cry of pain.

The sounds, and the sight of the automatic falling at his feet, filled me with a kind of crazy exultation. In that instant I felt huge, twice his size, a great dark looming presence hurtling toward him at flank speed. Another sound came out of me—laughter, maybe—when I saw him drop to his knees, scrabble for the gun with his left hand. It didn't matter what he did now. All the maneuvering, all the sly stalking was finished; the hunt was over. And the quarry wasn't Grady, it wasn't me, it was *him*.

Then I was on him. Then he was mine.

I slammed into him while he was on his knees; hit him with my arms and body and my own knees, and bowled him over backward across Grady's inert form. He grunted, then squealed with pain when my weight came down on his broken arm; bucked and kicked his legs to roll me off. I tried to hit

him in the face, hurt him, stun him, but the way he was
squirming and kicking I couldn't get any leverage. He gouged
at my eyes with his good hand, dug the heel of his shoe into
my thigh hard enough to put us into a roll. Another squeal,
then he was loose and starting to crawl away. Going after the
gun, or if he couldn't get to that, the tire iron.

He was scuttling like a crab, digging his left hand into the
dead brown earth, his right arm dangling crookedly, when I
pitched myself at his backside, got grips on his belt and his ass
and hauled him down. Drove a knee into his back . . . but he
was writhing, twisting, and I lost my balance and fell off to one
side. He pulled free again, set off scuttling again. This time I
caught one of his trailing legs, turned it, and he flopped over
onto his dead arm, yelling. I got hold of his other arm and the
shoulder of his jacket, but I couldn't stop him from blindly
rolling a second time . . . right up over the earth wrinkle,
feet first onto the steep drop above the gravel pit.

As soon as he felt himself starting to slide, he screwed over
onto his belly and dug desperately at the ground with his feet
and crippled arm. But he couldn't stop his momentum; what
stopped it was me, my two-handed grip on his left arm and
shoulder. His weight yanked me up against the wrinkle, but I
had my knees down and my shoetips dragging deep into the
earth and I was able to hang on to him and keep myself from
being pulled up and over.

And there we were, me sprawled across the wrinkle and
him hanging at a sharp angle below, both of us belly down
with our faces so close I could smell his sweat and the residue
of the bacon and eggs he'd had for breakfast.

He was the first to move, working frantically with his feet,
searching for enough purchase to propel himself upward. Fu-
tile: his feet weren't enough. He needed at least one hand and
arm, and he couldn't use either of his. It did not take him long
to realize this; to understand that he couldn't save himself,
that it was all up to me. I saw the knowledge come into his
face, dull the bright glaze of malice in his eyes.

"Pull me up," he said.

Sure, pull him up. The fight was out of him, most of it anyway; and if it wasn't, he was no match for me with that busted arm. Pull him up, clip him once or twice, go get the gun: easy. So hurry up, do it, before the strain pops one of your shoulder sockets. Pull him up, take him to the law, be done with him. Not my worry anymore. The cops, the courts . . . yeah . . . and a high-powered defense lawyer saying *"where's the evidence that my client murdered Mr. Savarese and set fire to his warehouse did you see him do it can you place him at the scene no? well neither can anyone else and as for Ms. Haas how do you know he intended to murder her on that hilltop or anywhere else she was overwrought even suicidal because he broke off their affair and he struck her to prevent her from harming herself picked her up in his arms to save her life not take it and you attacked him I submit you're the one who should be on trial here for aggravated assault. . . ."* and she wouldn't testify against him, not her . . . and all the things he'd done, to Arlo Haas, to Grady, to Kerry (Kerry!), to me, to any number of others . . . and if he got off scot-free, or even if he went to prison for a few years, he'd go right back to work at his trade and others would be hurt, more victims, unwilling victims, we don't care enough about the *victims. . . .*

"Pull me up," he said again.

One second. Two. Three. Four.

"Pull me up!"

I let go of him.

I just . . . let go.

Chapter **23**

HOW DO YOU rationalize a thing like that, an act of what society and society's laws consider to be murder? How do you come to terms with it?

The answer to both questions: You don't.

You don't rationalize it, you don't look for justification, you don't lie to yourself. It wasn't an accident; it wasn't the strain that caused you to let go. You did it deliberately, with a certain amount of malice aforethought, because in that moment of reckoning you saw no other choice according to *your* moral standards, *your* definition of justice. Society and society's laws don't matter. It isn't between you and society, this thing you did. It's between you and God, and He is the only judge who matters.

You don't come to terms with it either. How can you? You don't let yourself think about it at all; you don't dare let yourself think about it. Nor do you talk about it. Ever. To anyone, under any circumstances.

It happened, it's over. And you get on with your life.

* * *

BLACKWELL, THOMAS. Alias. Other known aliases: Jack King, Thomas Queen, Jack Brown, David Jones, Oliver Thomas, Peter Montana. Real name: Vincent Kenneth Tinney. Born in Brooklyn; 37 years of age. Father, Bertram Tinney (now deceased), was a teamster with loose Mob ties, mostly as a low-level enforcer for the loan sharks.

Juvenile record, beginning at age 15: Car theft, two arrests; breaking and entering, one arrest; malicious mischief, one arrest; arson, one arrest. Two years in a state reformatory on the arson charge: setting fire to a high school gymnasium, for which he was paid fifty dollars by four other youths.

Adult record: Two arrests, Arson One. *(Any person who willfully and maliciously sets fire to or burns or causes to be burned or who aids, counsels or procures the burning of any dwelling or house, whether occupied, unoccupied or vacant, or any kitchen, shop, barn, stable or other outhouse that is parcel thereof, or belonging to or adjoining thereto, whether the property of himself or of another, shall be guilty of Arson in the first degree, and upon conviction thereof, be sentenced to the penitentiary for not less than two nor more than twenty years.)* No convictions in either case; insufficient evidence. In the second of the two, a fire at a factory in the Bronx, two derelicts using a storage room for shelter had died of burns and smoke inhalation.

One arrest, Arson Two. *(Any person who willfully and maliciously sets fire to or burns or causes to be burned, or who aids, counsels or procures the burning of any building or structure of whatsoever class or character, whether the property of himself or of another, not included or described in the preceding section, shall be guilty of Arson in the second degree, and upon conviction thereof, be sentenced to the penitentiary for not less than one nor more than ten years.)* Conviction in this case; sentenced to five years in Sing Sing prison. Served full term, 1976–1981.

No arrests, state or federal, since his release.

M.O.: Favors chemical combustibles as incendiary mechanism. Potassium chlorate, sugar, and sulfuric acid; or potassium permanganate and glycerine; or metallic potassium and carbide. Favors water-ignition device, usually a condom or other rubber product in which a tiny hole is made with a pin. Also known to have used plastic explosives, traces of which were found by investigators from S.F.F.D.'s Arson Task Force in the remains of Savarese Importing's warehouse.

Psychological profile: Loner with almost fanatical desire for privacy, one reason for his use of numerous aliases. According to prison psychiatrist, a clinical sociopath with repressed psychotic tendencies. Considered to be dangerous in the extreme when cornered or threatened.

Habits: Moves frequently from place to place within a city or area and often from state to state. Prefers to live in small, quiet, moderately expensive hotels. Maintains few underworld contacts and has none of the common underworld vices. Heterosexual; prefers the company of respectable women whose habit patterns approximate his own.

Suspected recent activities: Moved from East Coast to West Coast within two years of his release from Sing Sing. Believed to be the number-one torch for a well-organized, Los Angeles-based arson ring specializing in industrial fires.

Official cause of death: Fracture of the axis or second cervical vertebra—professionally known as the Hangman's Fracture—as a result of a fall at South Valley Gravel Company, San Bernado, Monterey County, California.

Coroner's verdict: Death by accident and misadventure during alleged commission of a felony.

GRADY HAAS DID NOT react when I revived her on that wind-torn hilltop and told her the man she'd known as Jack King was dead. I said we'd struggled for the gun and he had lost his footing and fallen into the quarry, but I had the feeling she sensed the truth. She let me lead her down out of the hills and back to her father's house, but she would not look at me or speak to me. It was as if I, too, no longer existed for her.

She refused to tell the authorities what had happened between her and her lover to precipitate her flight from San Francisco and his hunt for her. She sang them the same lyrics of self-pity she'd sung for me: *It doesn't matter. I don't care. Leave me alone.* After a while, because Vincent Kenneth Tinney was dead, and because there was nothing else they could do, they obeyed her wishes—they left her alone.

If they'd worked at it, or if I had, we might have been able to do more than guess at the reasons. But why bother? Tinney was dead, Savarese was dead, Grady might as well be dead. She'd written the lyrics and they were true, with slight variations, to the very end.

It doesn't matter.

Who cares?

Leave it alone.

I STAYED IN THE SALINAS VALLEY for two days, as much to rest my sad old bones as for official reasons, and on both days I visited Arlo Haas in the hospital. That was once more than his daughter went to see him—and I stayed longer than she, both times. The second stroke had not left him permanently paralyzed, as the Vargases had feared. Eventually he would be able to go back to his farm, to continue to fend for himself. But the fending wouldn't last long, I thought. He was a changed man, a hollow man: He had lost his daughter, completely and irrevocably, and he knew it.

He didn't care anymore either.

GRADY WENT HOME to San Francisco. Back to her apartment, back to her job at Intercoastal Insurance, back to her carefully structured existence. Maybe one day she would begin living again, but I doubted it. Maybe one day she would find the courage—no, the cowardice—to destroy herself. But most likely she would just go on as she was, wearing her pain like widow's weeds, until she was old and withered and it was Father Time that finally did her in.

I didn't care anymore, one way or another.

EBERHARDT AND BOBBIE JEAN have patched things up. They're dating again, probably sleeping together again, but neither of them is talking about marriage. Not yet. Kerry thinks they will, soon, and that they'll be man and wife before the end of the year. I hope she's right.

Eb and I have patched things up, too—more or less. But it's still there between us, the things we said to each other that afternoon at his house, the punch in the belly that had ended it. Like a wall that neither of us seems able to tear down. We're cordial to each other at the office but we don't talk like we used to, we don't joke or laugh much; and we don't go out and have a few beers together after work. We don't get together socially at all, even though Kerry and Bobbie Jean are still fast friends.

Kerry says this will change, too, that it's only a temporary situation. She says Eb and I have been friends too long to let a small rift widen into an unbridgeable chasm. She says he needs me and I need him and down deep we both know it and it won't be long before we're compelled to admit it to each other. She says I'll still be best man at his wedding.

I hope she's right.

VINCENT KENNETH TINNEY'S FACE haunts my sleep.

I see it as it was in those last few seconds, the only time I ever saw it up close—tanned cheeks slick with sweat, lips drawn back, eyes wide and dark and evil. I see the arrogance in it, born of the certainty that I will pull him up, save him, because that's what men like me, the straight arrows, the poor honest fools, believe is the right thing to do. I see the arrogance fade and the terror take its place as he stares into *my* face, sees what it is *I* believe. I see his face fall away from me at last, grow smaller while the terror somehow grows larger in my perception, until he is gone.

I see all of that, and I hear him scream.

I will see his face and hear his scream for the rest of my life. But I will also remember the evil, as I remember the look of Kerry lying bloody and unconscious on my closet floor, and what it was like inside that burning warehouse, and Arlo Haas hollow and alone in his hospital bed—and something Haas said to me about the man who was after his daughter: "I'll serve him up hot to God or the devil, whichever wants him, and take my own chances when the time comes."

I am not sorry for what I did.

If I could relive that day, those hours, that last decisive moment with Vincent Kenneth Tinney—I would serve him up hot again.